INVITATION TO
DEATH

BRYAN SMITH

This one's for mom.

Other titles by Bryan Smith

ONE
DECEMBER 25, 2020

THE FIRST GUEST TO ARRIVE that Christmas evening, with perhaps a half hour of diminishing daylight remaining, was Bradley Winthorpe. The time was shortly after 5 p.m. After a long and harrowing drive up a narrow and winding road high up in the mountains, he stopped his 1969 Citroen DS 21 short of the entrance to the property he was visiting. The mountain road ended here. One could go no farther or turn around without entering the property grounds. The road was that narrow. He couldn't imagine a vehicle much larger than the Citroen making it up here safely. Two vehicles traveling in opposite directions along the same narrow lane would encounter an even thornier dilemma, though he supposed advance planning on the part of the property owner much reduced the likelihood of that happening. It was impossible to access the private road without first passing through a locked gate using a one-time entrance code. His code had been included with his invitation to tonight's private, exclusive event.

Now, as he sat in his idling vehicle with his foot held firmly on the brake pedal, he faced another gate. This one stood wide open, presumably because no one who wasn't supposed to be here would have made it this far anyway. A tall iron fence with pointy tips atop each of its slats surrounded the large estate, which was ringed by a dense forest. Above the ornate gate was an arched piece of custom wrought iron art spelling out the words *Raven's Reach*.

INVITATION TO DEATH

The massive manor house was visible at the end of a long, curving drive, which looped back around in this direction from the front of the house. A huge statue fountain was situated in the center of the large patch of open ground between the looping halves of the drive. The statue was of an ominous-looking cloaked figure sitting atop a horse rearing up on its back legs. The fountain was dry. Bradley had a hunch many years had passed since it'd last been operational.

He remained where he was a while longer, holiday music playing at low volume on the radio. Several full minutes passed while he lingered in hesitation and listened to Bing Crosby croon "White Christmas". He saw no other cars parked at the top of the long drive, nor did he see any parked anywhere else on the property. There were a few outlying buildings on the grounds, all of which looked larger than the average middle-class home. He supposed at least one might be a guest house, but the remaining buildings likely served other purposes. The one furthest away looked like a greenhouse.

No lights were on in any of the outlying buildings, adding an additional layer of creepiness to an already high overall creep factor. Also not helping matters was the total absence of any visible human presence on the property. No one was out walking about on the grounds. Nearly all the windows of the main house were also dark, lending the place an even eerier atmosphere as daytime continued giving way to dusk. A few lights, however, were visible on the ground floor, albeit only in the windows immediately adjacent to the front door. In that moment, the presence of those few lights was the only thing keeping him from zipping through the open gate, quickly turning around, and getting away from this place as fast as he could. Someone was in there. That's what those lights meant. They were in there and waiting for him.

A lot about this situation didn't feel right. Just the sight of the imposing manor itself was enough to send shivers running up his spine. From his research, he knew Raven's Reach was incredibly old, having been constructed in the latter part of the 18th century, right after the end of the Revolutionary War. Thanks to Wikipedia, he knew a lot about the origins of the estate. Its construction was commissioned by a wealthy shipping magnate named John Henry Thornton III. Though not technically a Founding Father of the United States, he moved in the same social circles. His fortune was one of the largest in the country at the time and was built on the backs of countless less fortunate people. Raven's Reach remained the property of the Thornton family for nearly three-quarters of a century, until certain heirs failed to produce offspring and the bloodline died out.

The question of who owned it now was a mystery. He'd tried every trick he could think of to unearth the property holder's name to no avail. Normally that sort of thing was a matter of public record, but apparently not in this case, a fact that added to the intrigue but also increased his wariness. Clearly *someone* owned it. Those lights and the invitation he'd received were proof enough of that.

Bradley shook his head and nervously drummed his fingers along the steering wheel rim. "That's a haunted house if I've ever seen one. No way am I going in there."

This was what his gut told him quite adamantly.

Leave.

Leave right fucking now.

And he might have done exactly that if not for two things, the first of those being the dreadful current state of his finances. Not long ago he'd been worth millions. Not elite level super-rich, but rich enough to make him think he could climb much higher. By making the right moves and with just a bit of luck, he truly believed he might one day find himself rubbing elbows with the likes of Bezos and Gates. Unfortunately, he ignored the advice of some well-paid and intelligent financial advisors and over-invested in several iffy ventures. One by one, like a shaky house of cards, those investments turned out bad.

Now he was all but penniless.

The invitation to tonight's event—the nature of which remained a mystery—arrived in the mail at the end of November. It rested now—sans envelope—on the passenger seat of the Citroen. He snatched it up and once again read the words imprinted on it in a cursive script on thick card stock.

You are cordially invited to spend an evening at enchanting Raven's Reach Manor on December 25, 2020. As part of an exclusive, hand-picked group of entrepreneurs and thought leaders, you will receive the sum of one million American dollars for staying overnight with us. No commitment beyond your attendance is required to receive this sum. All you need do is merely show up and experience our special, one-of-a-kind presentation. We understand this invitation may be met with skepticism. Please accept the enclosed check as a good-faith gesture and inducement for your attendance. This money is yours to keep whether you accept this invitation or not. Please see enclosed note for RSVP instructions and additional details.

INVITATION TO DEATH

Had this invitation arrived in the midst of the previous year's holiday season, he would have immediately dismissed it as an obvious scam unworthy of his attention. This year, however, was nothing like last year. Though he outwardly maintained the trappings and appearance of wealth, in truth he'd become a desperate man eager to grab hold of anything that looked even vaguely like a lifeline. The check included with the invitation was made out in the amount of $25,000. He examined it closely for signs of fakery, but found nothing obvious to indicate it was anything other than genuine. It appeared drawn from a real account from a real bank. The account name was Raven's Reach LLC. Some phone inquiries quickly confirmed these basic facts. The sum was far from a fortune and would put only the slightest of dents in his overall debt load, but it was nothing to sneeze at either. He deposited the check and made plans to attend the mysterious event at Raven's Reach Manor.

The note accompanying the invitation included a phone number. He called the number and used a numerical code to RSVP. After entering the code, a recorded message played, in which a monotone male voice informed him of a strict arrival time for the event and instructed him to bring along no more than one guest. He was also told not to speak of the event to anyone not also invited. Any violations of this edict would result in a rescinding of the invitation. Bradley didn't see how that could be enforced short of monitoring his every communication or interaction, online or in the flesh. As unlikely as this seemed, however, he chose not to speak of the event to anyone, a resolve that intensified the moment the check cleared. It seemed he had a real shot at collecting an easy million dollars and he didn't want to take even the slightest chance of botching the opportunity.

Bringing along a guest might have allayed some of his biggest fears regarding the highly unusual nature of this trip. No one liked facing the unknown alone, after all, especially under such creepy circumstances. He chose to go it alone anyway for the simple reason of wanting to limit knowledge of his impending windfall. This was mostly because Bradley wasn't just in debt to impersonal financial institutions, where the worst that could happen was being forced into declaring bankruptcy. Unfortunately, he was also in debt to other lenders. Shadier people employed by organizations not bound by the constraints of law. So this was the other reason he'd come to this remote location on this windswept, chilly evening.

That million dollars might just save his life.

In the end, he had no choice, really.

Turning back would be an act of surrender.

He flicked the invitation away. Then, with a final pensive sigh, he took his foot off the brake pedal and drove through the open gate. In less than a minute, he arrived at the top of the looping drive, where he put the Citroen in park but kept the engine running a few moments longer as he stared at the closed door and waited to see if someone would come out to greet him.

When that did not happen, he cut the engine off and got out of the car. After another moment of frowning at the manor's closed front door over the roof of the Citroen, he went around to the trunk, opened it, and took out his overnight bag. Packed inside were two Ziploc bags containing toiletries, one change of leisure clothes suitable for wearing during daytime hours at the home of an obscenely wealthy person, and his gun, a Walther PPK. The gun was something he did not expect to have to use, but having it handy helped with maintaining his peace of mind. In the event he'd been invited here for some sinister reason—a thing he still mostly viewed as unlikely— he would at least have some form of protection.

He closed the trunk lid, grabbed his suit bag from a hook inside the car, and took another look around before approaching the manor. Seeing no obvious alternate place to stow the Citroen, he had no choice but to leave it parked at the top of the drive for the time being. His expectation when visiting a place like Raven's Reach was that a butler or some other servant would, after greeting him at the door and ushering him into the house, take his keys and park his vehicle in a big garage somewhere on the property. He supposed that might yet still happen after he knocked on the door, but the lonely outward vibe of the place made him doubt it.

Sighing, he climbed the steps to the porch. A cast iron door knocker in the shape of a wolf's head was affixed to the center of the sturdy oak door. Hanging from the wolf's mouth was a heavy iron ring. Bradley gripped the ring in his fingers and thumped it against the door three times, an action resulting in a resonant, ominous-sounding tone he suspected was similar to what one would hear when knocking on the lid of a rich man's expensive casket. He stepped back and shivered while he waited, disquieted by how readily the death and funeral metaphors kept coming to mind.

Some minutes passed. No one came to open the door, nor did he hear anyone moving about inside. No footsteps. No voices. Nothing at all. The time that elapsed was more than enough for him to start getting antsy. He didn't want to be that obnoxious person who got impatient and knocked repeatedly and insistently, but after more than five minutes passed, he felt he had no choice but to try again. This time he banged the heavy iron ring against the door with a little more force, and this time those deep, resonant tones were almost like cracks of thunder.

He stepped back and waited again. Five more minutes elapsed without anyone coming to the door. Six minutes. Seven.

Finally he'd had enough. "Fuck this."

Short of breaking in or throwing rocks at a window, he didn't know what else to do. He didn't want to stand here and wait all night like a fool. Nor did he wish to walk the grounds of the place in search of someone to help him. In the time he'd been standing here, the wind had picked up and more of those little white flakes were swirling about.

"Fuck."

After casting one last look around and still not encountering evidence of anyone else on the property, he tried the door handle and was surprised to find it yielding to the pressure. The door creaked loudly as it swung inward. Bradley gave it a hard push, the louder creaking sound making him grimace as the door opened wider. He paused on the threshold and poked his head around the edge of the door as he got his first look of the interior of the place.

"Wow."

He winced at the sound of his own voice, which sounded amplified in what was easily the largest foyer he'd ever seen in a private residence. Twin spiral staircases at each side of the vast space led to the second of the manor's three floors, each branching off toward a different wing of the estate. The space between the staircases led to a wide hallway and numerous other rooms. Two other hallways to the left and right of the foyer entrance led to still more rooms and unknown other parts of the manor's first floor. Bulbs from a large chandelier hanging overhead made the marble floor tiles gleam brightly.

The only piece of furniture in the foyer was a small round table situated in the middle of the space. Atop the table was what looked like a Christmas stocking. Just that and nothing else. A name inscribed in glued-on glitter was visible on the white cuff of the stocking. He had a hunch what the name might be but couldn't read it from the threshold.

Still feeling a great wariness, he moved a few steps deeper into the foyer without closing the door behind him. The creep factor here was going up instead of down, and he hoped to maintain an easy, quick way out should the need for fast retreat arise. He was about halfway between the door and the little round table when he heard the door creak behind him. By the time he turned around, the door was clicking shut. His heart pounding, he ran to it and tried the handle. It would not budge.

"Oh, shit." He was panting and his voice rose higher in pitch and volume as he uttered his next words. "What the fuck is happening here?"

His heart was still racing.

He was officially scared.

Scurrying about, he quickly checked the windows adjacent to the door. He saw no one on the porch or running away across the grounds, and he was fairly certain he'd moved fast enough to catch sight of anyone before they could disappear. There'd been no sound of footsteps on the marble tiles behind him either. He could only conclude the door had been closed by electronic means from a remote location. At this thought, the paranoia percolating inside him went into overdrive. Somebody was watching him. How else would they have known when to close the door? He cast his gaze all about, searching the foyer for signs of hidden cameras. He didn't find anything, but that meant nothing. High-end spy cameras these days could be as small as a pin-point.

His attention returned to the stocking on the table. He hurriedly approached the table and saw his guess was right. The name spelled out in glitter was his own.

Bradley.

The stocking looked empty at first glance. A closer look, however, revealed the corner of a folded piece of paper sticking out of it. He might easily have missed this because barely a half-inch of paper was visible. Setting his overnight bag on the floor, he plucked the piece of paper from the stocking and unfolded it, finding a note addressed to him, which appeared to have been written on a slightly malfunctioning old typewriter. A couple of its keys had repeatedly struck the paper at a lower level than the others, resulting in a few sentences he had to read multiple times in order to make sense of them.

The note read as follows:

INVITATION TO DEATH

Bradley,

Welcome to Raven's Reach. As you must have deduced by now, the event to which you have been invited is quite out of the ordinary. Once inside the manor, you will not be allowed to leave prior to sunrise tomorrow. Please do not be alarmed! This is but a minor inconvenience necessary to facilitate successful completion of tonight's special presentation. Your room for the night is on the second floor of the eastern wing. A card with your name on it will mark the room.

Two important points for you, Bradley. Once you enter your room, you must not leave it until notified, otherwise you will be disqualified from your chance to earn a million dollars. Also, you must leave the keys to your Citroen and the Walther PPK you brought with you behind. Place these items in the stocking and leave the stocking on the table. Again, if you do not do this, you will be disqualified. Your property will be returned to you on the morrow. Please be assured the prize you came to collect is very real. One million dollars is within your grasp should you be willing to abide by these simple guidelines.

And that was it.

No signature, which was hardly a surprise.

Bradley read through the note twice more before shaking his head and sighing in exasperation. The situation was seeming sketchier by the moment. It was clear this whole thing had been set up by someone who was not quite right in the head. He could be facing real danger by remaining here. On the other hand, real danger definitely awaited him back out there in the regular world. Without that million dollars, he'd have virtually no hope of getting those mob guys off his back. There was no real choice here. This was a chance he had to take, sketchy or not.

"Fuck."

He retrieved his travel bag from the floor and set it on the little table. The Walther was tucked away in a side compartment. He unzipped the pouch, removed the weapon, and stuffed it in the stocking as instructed, along with the keys to his car.

While his fear of the mob was absolutely a big factor in his decision to go along with the demands of the letter writer, an even bigger one was the writer's knowledge of his gun. There were all sorts of creepy implications inherent in that fact alone. He'd told no one where he was going for the weekend, much less said anything about bringing the gun along, which meant the person behind this so-called "exclusive event" had someone watching him virtually at all times. They maybe even had eyes inside his house in the form of cameras. They might have hacked into his computer or phone. A person like that, playing along was the only sensible move.

Not playing along might make them mad.

Making them mad might get a person killed.

Sighing heavily, Bradley set the stocking back down on the table, zipped up his bag, and went up to the second floor in search of his room.

TWO

TINA AND NINA MARTINSON ARRIVED in the small town of Thornton at around four in the afternoon that Christmas day. They were in a rented Ford minivan picked up from the Hertz station at the airport over in the much larger city of Rutledge. Because Thornton was three hours away by highway under optimal conditions, they hit the road right away. Tina took the wheel because her twin sister was a lousy driver even though she didn't believe it.

Didn't matter if Nina didn't believe it, though. Her record of speeding tickets and assorted other moving violations spoke for itself. She drove aggressively at unsafely fast speeds, whereas Tina drove judiciously fast while exercising all necessary caution. Not a single citation on her record in the last ten years, a not unimportant factor for siblings in regular need of transporting corpses to rural dump sites far from home. Thus Tina always drove when they were out doing something important or potentially dangerous. That was the rule and it was iron-clad.

The sisters were serial killers.

They took up their favorite hobby almost by accident when they were sophomores in college, almost twenty years earlier. A night out with some girlfriends extended deep into the wee hours, with the numbers of their party gradually dwindling down to just three by the end of the evening. The sisters and their friend Gwendolyn stumbled out of a dive bar after last call and, being too drunk to drive, they began the long walk back toward campus, where Gwendolyn lived in a dorm. The apartment Tina and Nina shared was much closer, albeit still university adjacent. Though the sisters were quite inebriated, they were better at pacing themselves over the course of a long night of imbibing than their friend, who was close to blind drunk. After stumbling precariously along in her high heels for almost a mile, Gwendolyn asked the sisters if she could crash with them for the night.

The sisters said yes, of course.

What else would true friends do?

Up in their second-floor apartment, they spent some time lounging about and having some more drinks. Tina had nothing sinister in mind at that point. They'd had so many crazy evenings just like this one since the start of their college career. Getting up for those first morning classes in a few hours would be rough, but they'd get through it like always. In another night or two, they'd go out with the gang and do it all over again. They were normal college students doing normal college student things. It was a time-honored tradition passed down through the generations. Nothing more than that.

Until that moment when Gwendolyn announced she had to go pee. She got up and, once again wobbling precariously from the overabundance of strong alcohol flowing through her system, set off in the direction of the bathroom. If anything, the wobbling was even more pronounced than before. This despite being in her bare feet instead of those three-inch heels. Before she could make it out of the living room, she stumbled and banged her face against the edge of the partition separating the living room from the kitchen.

The sisters yelped and jumped up from their seats as their drunken friend dropped like a rock to the floor. Gwendolyn hit the floor on her side and flopped over onto her back. Nina was gibbering hysterically, saying the same three words ("Oh my God!") over and over in rapid succession while Tina knelt next to their friend and checked for a pulse. She detected one almost immediately, strong and steady. Their friend didn't seem to be in any immediate critical danger, but she'd been rendered unconscious by the hard knock to her head. Her eyes were open, but stared blankly up at the ceiling. Her nose was broken and steady trickles of blood leaked from her nostrils. The entire lower half of her face was already stained crimson. Those things, combined with the way her mouth was hanging open, made the girl look dead despite that strong pulse. Something about that impression triggered something primal inside Tina, transfixing her in a way nothing else had since a day five years earlier that had turned her young life upside down.

This was back in her high school days. She was home hours earlier than usual, otherwise she was sure she never would've been able to spy on her mother having sex with the neighbor boy. The boy's name was Saul. Saul was just two years older than Kathy Martinson's twin daughters. Tina remembered standing in the upstairs hallway that day with laser clarity. It was always there, that memory, lurking just behind the forefront of her conscious mind, rising up to taunt her again and again in the years that followed.

Tina loved and worshipped her father back then. He was her hero. Until that day, she'd believed her mother must feel the same way about the man. As she peered in through the narrow crack between door and doorframe, her mother was atop Saul, riding his cock with ferocious abandon. Saul's arms were stretched out behind him and tied to the headboard with scarves. His face was a bright scarlet from the way Kathy kept repeatedly slapping him. She called the boy names, too. Mean, filthy, vicious things, words unlike anything she'd ever heard her mother say before.

Tina was filled with confusion throughout this incident. Anger rose up inside her as she continued to watch, surprising her with its intensity. She wanted to run downstairs, grab a big knife from the kitchen, then burst in on them and stab each of them a hundred times. The fantasy image of bloody revenge was so vivid and compelling that for one vertigo-inducing moment she wavered on the brink of actually doing it. Instead, she retreated from the house in tears and didn't come home for hours. When she finally did return, Saul was gone and her dad was home. Kathy Martinson was bustling about the kitchen as she smilingly prepared the nightly family dinner. Outwardly, there was no trace of the foul-mouthed whore who'd fucked the neighbor boy with such shocking aggression. Tina never looked at her mother the same way after that. That smiling face was a lie. It was nothing more than a mask. Living under that roof for three more years was a grueling exercise in hiding smoldering resentment and barely repressed rage.

A corner of Tina's mouth twitched as she shook off the hurtful old memories. Her sister paced about and made more fretful noises, sounds that barely penetrated as Tina continued to stare at Gwendolyn's slack features with an odd kind of fascination, a feeling that made no sense to her in those first few minutes after the accident. Then it hit her, what that feeling was really about. She liked the way Gwendolyn looked lying there on the floor. Liked how she strongly resembled a corpse. It stirred something in her, an excitement that was at least partly sexual.

She didn't know what she was going to do until it happened. She closed Gwendolyn's mouth and covered it with her hand. With the fingers of her other hand, she pinched her nostrils shut.

Nina abruptly stopped pacing and gasped. "My God, Tina! What are you doing?"

Tina's voice was surprisingly calm as she replied. "Trying something."

Another gasp from her sister. "Trying something?" Nina's tone was incredulous. "It looks like you're trying to kill her."

Nina grunted. "I am."

"But . . . why?"

Tina didn't have an answer for that, not one she could clearly articulate in those moments. Before she could say anything at all, that blankness vanished from Gwendolyn's eyes as she awoke and fuzzily realized what was happening. The girl tried rolling away, but before she could, Tina quickly straddled her and held her in place. She squealed in fright beneath Tina's firmly pressing hand and then tried grabbing at Tina's long hair to yank her away.

Tina glared at her sister. "Grab her hands."

Their eyes met and for a moment Nina wavered in indecision. Tina had no idea what her sister might do. She might bolt from the apartment in search of a neighbor to help her. Or perhaps she'd call the police or even attempt to pull Tina away from the struggling girl.

The moment passed. None of those things happened.

Nina instead dropped to her knees, grabbed hold of Gwendolyn's slender wrists, and held her formerly flailing arms still. Gwendolyn's struggles continued for what felt like forever at the time, but probably wasn't more than a couple of minutes. Tina kept the girl's airways shut for at least another full minute after she stopped moving. Then she took her hands away from Gwendolyn's face and felt for a pulse.

There wasn't one.

Gwendolyn was dead. They'd killed her.

Both of them. Sisters working together.

They got up and had another drink, leaving Gwendolyn's body where it was on the floor.

"What now?" Nina asked.

She sounded calmer than Tina expected. "We finish our drinks and go to bed. In the morning, we call 911 and report finding our friend dead on the floor. We'll sound distraught. The cops and emergency people will show up and see how she had her accident. They'll think it killed her. A toxicology test will show how fucked up she was. We'll go on with our lives. The end."

A thoughtful pause ensued as Nina nodded. "They'd never believe we killed her anyway," she said at last, a hint of unexpected mirth in her voice. "We're nice girls."

After a moment, Tina giggled. "Yes. Yes, we are."

A short while after that, they did go to bed. When they awoke a few hours later, Tina called 911 and events transpired pretty much exactly as she'd envisioned. No one blamed them for Gwendolyn's death. It was just another of the countless unfortunate alcohol-related deaths that happened on college campuses all across the country every year.

A few months later, after the semester was over and the Gwendolyn incident was safely behind them, the sisters stalked and intentionally lured a victim to his demise for the first time. This time they were sober and careful, and they got away with it once again. Thus emboldened, they set out on a long career of killing, employing varying methods to keep things fresh and fun along the way. They'd been at it for nearly two full decades by the time their invitation to the event at Raven's Reach arrived in the mail.

Like Bradley Winthorpe, their initial reaction was deep skepticism. Not just skepticism, either. Women who lived the way they did and did the things they did naturally developed a highly evolved suspicion of when things weren't quite right. From the start, the invitation made both sisters feel as if someone was trying to lure them into a trap. Who might be behind it, however, was a complete mystery. Could be anyone related to their dozens of victims through the years. An especially determined individual, possibly, one who'd devoted much time, energy, and money into tracking them down. They'd always been so careful in the way they went about the business of killing, never leaving evidence behind, but slip-ups were always a danger. One could never tell when a fatal one might occur.

Thus why their original inclination was to ignore the invitation. They made no attempt to deposit or cash the check that was included. That the check was real was never in doubt. They simply wanted no part of this strange business.

Two weeks after the original invitation arrived, another one showed up in their mailbox. The second invitation arrived along with a padded envelope containing only an unlabeled DVD-R in a slim plastic case. Tina put the disc in their Blu-ray player and pushed play. The screen filled with an image of the sisters romping around naked inside a blood-spattered bedroom. They were laughing and gleeful, their bodies smeared with large splotches of drying crimson. At one point, Nina ceased romping long enough to ram a knife into the throat of the dead man on the bed. The screen went blank after two minutes filled with garish footage.

Tina grunted at the blank screen. "Well, shit."

Nina sounded more anxious. "What does it mean? How fucked are we?"

Instead of answering, Tina called the number included with the note that accompanied the second invitation to Raven's Reach, entering the one-time RSVP code. She put the phone on speaker and this time they heard a message clearly recorded especially for them. They were told the incriminating footage they'd watched was just the tip of the iceberg. There was a lot more of it. This evidence—every last bit of it—would be destroyed should they attend the gathering at Raven's Reach on the appointed day.

Otherwise, it would all be turned over to the police.

Like Bradley, they had no real choice.

Tina hit the appropriate buttons to confirm their acceptance of the invitation. She hung up and that was that. No more communication or threats from Raven's Reach. Two weeks of tentative calm ensued while they made plans to travel across the country and discussed what they might do if their dark secrets were revealed to the world. And now here they were, driving up that narrow and treacherous mountain road. More than once they feared the rented minivan would slide over the edge of the road and go tumbling down the side of the mountain.

A sudden catastrophe of that sort might not be the worst possible exit for the sisters, something Nina remarked upon as Tina held fast to the wheel and struggled to keep all four of the minivan's tires on relatively solid ground. "Think about it," she said, staring out the passenger side window at the steep slope below. "This fucking thing would tumble a long ways before landing down there in the valley. We'd be smashed into hamburger meat. There'd be maybe a few seconds of blinding pain and then it'd all be over. You have to admit, it'd beat the hell out of spending years or decades on death row."

Tina grimaced as she tilted the wheel a careful increment to the left to keep the minivan moving safely along the curving road. "Could you please stop with the fucking fatalism? We've talked about this. As long as we play along with whatever game is being played here, there's no reason to fear public exposure. If exposing us was all they wanted, they could have done that already. We're here for some other reason."

Nina nodded. "You're absolutely right, and there are several scary-as-fuck possibilities, the biggest one being revenge. This whole thing might have been organized by relatives of people we've killed. Could be we've been summoned here for a long night of torture and re-venge."

Tina sighed.

She was weary of hearing her sister recite the long list of dreadful possibilities and theories about what might happen tonight. Admit-tedly, many of them were disturbingly plausible, but nothing about what awaited them at Raven's Reach was certain yet. There was even a chance they'd been summoned here for reasons that might prove beneficial. After all, the check included with the invitation had cleared with no problem. Now each of them was twenty-five grand richer, minus travel fare and related purchases. It was a hefty sum to throw at people one only intended to kill.

Tina knew her sister's fears were not without foundation, but she wasn't overly worried about being tortured or murdered tonight, and it was mainly the money that made her feel that way. No, she was fairly certain something else was afoot here. It was even possible who-ever had summoned them was some wealthy uber-elite weirdo fasci-nated by serial killers, one who'd used their limitless resources to identify them and document their work.

A fan, in other words.

In that case, tonight might wind up being one of the most exciting and interesting nights of their lives.

Around another bend, the road went into a slight rise, and in an-other few moments the open gate outside Raven's Reach came into view. Like Bradley less than twenty minutes before them, they spent some moments lingering outside the gate, the minivan's engine idling as they stared up at the impressively sprawling massive estate.

Nina audibly swallowed a lump in her throat. "Um . . . wow."

Tina chuckled. "Yeah. That's about the size of it. Fucking wow."

She steered the minivan through the open gate and drove up to the top of the looping drive.

On their way up there, Nina leaned over and frowned at the fountain statue. "What the fuck is that supposed to be? Is that dude on the horse the Grim Reaper or some shit?"

Tina shrugged. "Don't know. Don't care. It's old as fuck and therefore nothing to do with us."

Bradley's Citroen was nowhere in sight as she pulled up and parked alongside the manor's porch. The sisters would not see or know about Bradley or any of the other invitees for hours to come. They did, however, go through a similar process of discovery and feeling out after exiting the minivan. This included surveying what they could see of the vast property and feeling the eerie, heavy emptiness of the place. The lack of any other visible human presence made Tina feel like an explorer of some lost and forgotten land. The manor was monstrously huge. Approaching it felt like walking up to the mouth of a dragon's cavernous lair.

After a wasted few minutes of dithering, they belatedly discovered they were meant to enter the manor of their own accord. Once inside, they discovered stockings with their names inscribed in glued-on glitter resting on the same little table Bradley had approached only a short while ago. Inside the stockings were notes addressed to each of them.

After reading the notes, the sisters exchanged worried looks before reluctantly opening up their travel bags and removing the knives they'd purchased en route to Raven's Reach after landing in Rutledge. These were hunting knives with long, serrated edges. The sisters had killed numerous people over the years utilizing ones that were almost identical.

Nina spoke in hushed tones as she angrily shoved her folded knife deep into the stocking. "I don't like this. How the fuck could they have known about the knives?"

Tina didn't have an answer for that. Not one that would calm her sister's raging sense of paranoia, at least.

With the knives stashed away as instructed, the sisters zipped up their bags and went up to their rooms, where they would await whatever might happen next with steadily rising trepidation.

THREE

OF ALL THE INVITEES TO the mysterious event at Raven's Reach, Harlan Ross was one of just two who refused to respond to the invitation he received regardless of the multiple attempts at intimidation directed at him. He was one of several who initially thought he was the target of an attempted scam. The invitation and the check promptly went into his office shredder, after which he didn't think of it again until a second invitation arrived just five days later.

The second invitation was stamped with the word URGENT in bold red letters across the front of the envelope. He opened it and again found another check for a not insignificant sum. This time he gave the check more than a cursory examination and decided it might be real after all. It had all the earmarks of the genuine article. Regardless, it mattered not one whit to Harlan, who'd inherited a large sum from his parents following their fluke deaths in an automobile accident several years earlier. In the time since then, he'd invested wisely and was now a man of considerable wealth. It would take a lot more than a mere hundred grand to impress or lure him.

The invitation itself was terser and more sternly worded this time. It read:

Dear Mr. Harlan Ross,

Your presence at the December 25th event at Raven's Reach is required. You must respond via electronic RSVP within the next forty-eight hours. Please call

the number on the included note and enter the provided one-use code when
prompted.

   Sincerely,

   Raven's Reach

Despite its brevity, several things rankled him about this note. Primary among them was the use of words like "required" and "must", which intimated he had no actual choice in the matter. The wording implied a command rather than a polite request. It also not-so-subtly implied some vague form of threat should he fail to do as the sender of the note desired. The stated short time frame for response also struck Harlan as designed to make him anxious as the hours ticked away and the deadline approached. Then there was the note's closing valediction, signed not with a person's name but the name of the manor itself, which made it obnoxiously impersonal. He'd be damned if he'd give anyone hiding in a cloak of anonymity the time of day.

Once again, the invitation and check went into his shredder.

When he returned from his daily walk the next day, he found a letter-sized envelope taped to the front door of his house. His name was printed in ink in large block letters on the front of the envelope. It didn't take a genius to see the letter (or whatever it was) had not been sent through the regular U.S. mail. Instead, someone associated with or hired by the people at Raven's Reach had brazenly walked right up to his door and put it where he'd be sure to see it. Even before he opened it, he knew it was their doing because the printed letters "RR" appeared in the bottom right corner of the envelope.

After looking around to see if he was being watched (he wasn't, as best he could tell), Harlan took the envelope back into his house. His fingers shook slightly as he tore it open and extracted the single sheet of copy paper inside. The note was again brief, but this time it was handwritten. There was a phone number. He recognized it from the previous notes. There was also a new one-use RSVP code. Other than those things, the note consisted of one bluntly short sentence. *"Call or else."*

Harlan gaped at the note in spluttering disbelief for several minutes before he could even begin to organize his thoughts. When he finally was able to begin thinking in a clear way again, the overriding emotion he felt was not fear but indignation. The sheer chutzpah of these people was confounding and close to inconceivable. Some level of fear had been there in those first stupefied moments, yes, but it was quickly washed away by his surging anger. This affront would not stand. No way. No how.

Instead of calling the number on the note, Harlan called a private detective whose services he'd engaged in the aftermath of his parents' untimely demise. The police disagreed, but he'd always found the circumstances of their "accident" suspicious. The detective didn't turn up anything, but he'd done good, thorough work. He was expensive, but worth it. After hearing him out, the detective agreed to take on this new case. He seemed confident he'd get to the bottom of whatever was behind these acts of intimidation. For an extra fee, he'd even lean on them extra hard and scare them off for good. Harlan cheerfully paid for this additional service.

Feeling relieved after his conversation with the detective, Harlan went about his daily business and did not allow himself to be troubled by the matter. He scarcely thought of it at all until the detective's personal assistant phoned him two days later. She was sobbing as she told him about her employer's unfortunate accident. He was in a coma and not expected to recover. Even through her tears, the woman admirably strove for professionalism. She offered to put Harlan in touch with another detective. He declined and hung up on her in mid-sentence.

Clearly this was a far more serious matter than he'd realized. These people not only meant business, they were not above using violence to get what they wanted. He now suspected they would not relent until he acceded to their wishes. At that point, many would have buckled beneath the pressure, giving in to the demand that he call the number provided.

Harlan Ross, however, was made of sterner stuff than that.

More determined than ever not to be forced into doing something he didn't want to do, he went out the same day and bought a gun. The Glock 9mm accompanied him everywhere from that point forward.

Two days of no contact from anyone representing Raven's Reach elapsed after he bought the gun. Then came the afternoon when someone knocked on his door. It was a strident knocking, loud and insistent. He was in his study at the time, smoking his pipe and reading a new biography on Sir Arthur Conan Doyle, and the loud knocking caused him to jump in his chair. The thick book slid from his fingers and dropped to the floor. He picked it up and saw that the impact with the floor had caused a corner of the hardback volume to become noticeably dented.

An angry scowl curved his face as the knocking resumed. He set the book on his desk, wedged the pipe in a corner of his mouth, and retrieved his new gun from its place next to his vintage Olivetti typewriter. After clearing his throat and puffing himself up sufficiently, he strode through his house with a purposeful quickness, opened his front door, and stuck the barrel of the gun in the face of a man he'd never seen before.

"Now look here, you son of a bitch," Harlan said, speaking as clearly as he could manage around the pipe wedged in his mouth. "I've had enough of this nonsense. You slink on back to whatever hole you crawled out of, and when you get there, call your bosses and tell them the next emissary they send will be leaving in a body bag. You may also tell them to fuck off, and furthermore, to keep fucking off for all eternity. Am I making myself perfectly clear?"

The man standing on his porch was tall and fit. He wore a cream-colored trench coat and a fedora, the brim pulled low over his eyes. A long and livid scar traced down along the left side of his face, continuing just below the jawline. Once upon a time, Harlan figured, someone had come at this man with the intent of killing him, laying his flesh open down to the bone with a large and nastily sharp blade. He looked like a thug from some old-time Hollywood movie. The muzzle of the Glock hovered three inches from the tip of his nose. He stared blankly past it at Harlan, his expression cold and unreadable, betraying no emotion of any kind. Not anger. Not fear.

Nothing at all.

For a fleeting moment, Harlan found himself troubled by the possibility of this stranger having nothing at all to do with the bothersome pests at Raven's Reach. He might be here for some far more innocuous reason. Perhaps he was a neighbor from down the street in search of a wayward pet, or a door-to-door salesman looking to scam a quick buck. Maybe he was a cop with a fetish for old noir movies. Given that he couldn't remember the last time a salesman had knocked on his door, the cop scenario seemed more likely. Sure, it made sense. There might have been some new development in the case of the assault on the detective he'd hired and this man was here to ask some follow-up questions. Just as Harlan was beginning to believe the cop theory, however, the man started slowly backing away. Strange. A cop seemed likely to flash a badge, maybe even pull a gun of his own.

Instead, he smirked and said, "Nice pipe, Sherlock."

Harlan frowned.

What a strange thing to say . . .

After a few more backward steps, the man in the trench coat
turned away from him and began walking briskly away. By then Harlan knew the man was no police detective. A cop would at least have
identified himself as such. It was also readily apparent the man was
no regular citizen. An innocent person with no ill intent in mind
would at least have flinched upon unexpectedly encountering a gun
pointed at his face. This man had barely reacted. Harlan had a hunch
it was not the first time he'd found himself in such a position. The
man had come here to intimidate and harass him.

An impulse nearly sent Harlan chasing after the man. This time
he'd put the gun in his face again and demand answers. But Harlan
stayed where he was. Despite his display of bravado, he was not a
tough guy. Going after an obvious hardened thug would not be a wise
thing to do. So, instead, he watched as the man got into an old sedan
parked at the side of the street. The car was rust-flecked and painted
a faded shade of green. There was no license plate on the back. The
man started the car and drove slowly away.

Once it was out of sight, Harlan backed into his house and locked
the door. He stood there in the foyer a moment, staring at the closed
door, until he realized he was trembling all over. Taking the pipe from
his mouth, he wiped sweat from his forehead and made a soft sound
that was almost a whimper. This was clearly a delayed reaction to the
drama of the moment, now that the immediate danger had passed.
He took some deep breaths and tried to calm down. Once he had
himself relatively under control, he made a full circuit of his house,
upstairs and downstairs, making sure every window and door was
closed and locked. He pulled down shades and closed shutters over
windows, making it darker inside. The gloom unnerved him, so he
made another circuit of the house, turning on all the lights.

When he was satisfied he'd made the house as secure as he could,
he returned to his study and poured himself a stiff drink. He sat in
the comfortable chair behind his desk and took a single sip of bourbon. Then his gaze fell on the Doyle biography. His mind instantly
flashed back to the only words spoken by his visitor.

Nice pipe, Sherlock.

His mouth dropped slowly open as his mind was again engulfed
by paranoia. The reference to Doyle's most famous fictional creation
seemed like an awfully big coincidence. Had the man somehow

known what he was reading? He didn't see how that was possible unless a camera had been planted somewhere in his study. As soon as this thought crossed his mind, an exhaustive search of the room became inevitable. He looked everywhere. Pulled all his books down from the shelves. Peeked in every corner. Studied the ceiling. Examined every square inch of space.

Nothing.

Only after his search was finished did another, possibly more likely, explanation occur. The Doyle biography was a recent purchase. Harlan didn't like to buy books online. He preferred to make his reading choices only after physically handling the books in which he was interested. This one was picked out after nearly two hours of leisurely browsing at his preferred local book emporium only about a week ago. Someone might have been watching him the entire time. Someone employed by Raven's Reach. He hadn't been aware of any prolonged scrutiny by anyone while he was there, but he imagined a professional would know how to avoid being spotted. The timing was right. It fit. And the man uttering those words was making no random attempt at snark. The remark was designed to get under his skin.

And it had worked perfectly.

Harlan's next few days were fraught with anxiety. He stayed in his house nearly the entire time, afraid to even go outside long enough to check his mail. After two days of mail piling up, the mailman knocked on his door. Recognizing the man as his regular carrier when he looked at him through the peephole, he opened the door just long enough to snatch the pile of bills and junk mail from his hand before slamming the door shut and locking it again.

The days drifted by in a boozy blur for a bit until he realized a full week had passed with no further harassment or contact from Raven's Reach. No envelopes in the mail or taped to his door. No booming knocks on his door. Nothing at all. They were leaving him alone.

By then Christmas was just under a week away.

He began to relax.

Maybe they'd finally realized he couldn't be bullied into doing what they wanted.

More days passed.

Christmas Eve arrived.

He awoke around noon and spent some time watching Christmas movies on TV. They made him sad, reminding him of his own lack of close loved ones. His parents were dead. He had no siblings. He had a few friendly acquaintances, but none that were close. Because he was comfortably set for the rest of his life, he had no need of employment. He therefore had no co-workers with whom he might have become friendly. Once upon a time he'd been married to an emotionally cold woman, a miserable union that somehow dragged on for seven grim years. They'd last communicated almost a decade ago and he'd avoided all romantic entanglements since then. His was an almost entirely solitary existence and most of the time he was okay with it. Except for on certain days.

Holidays, mostly.

He switched from coffee to liquor early that afternoon and wound up passing out in front of the TV. When his eyes fluttered open a few hours later, he was groggy, but not so out of it that he didn't immediately realize there were other people in the room with him. They were clad in black with black ski masks over their heads. The black clothes were form-fitting, allowing him to easily tell one of the intruders was a woman. There were two of them. The woman had a gun and it was aimed at his face. Fear and adrenaline sped up his return to full consciousness. He tried rising up out of his recliner, but the man roughly shoved him back down.

"Time to go back to sleep, Sherlock," a gruff voice told him.

He recognized the voice.

A syringe materialized out of seemingly nowhere, clasped in the man's gloved hand. Harlan tried swatting it away as the dripping needle came arcing toward his neck, but the man grabbed his wrist with his free hand and twisted it away with ease. He felt a sharp, painful prick as the needle plunged into his neck. His head began to feel fuzzy again within moments as some strong drug started circulating through his system.

The man chuckled. "Good night, Sherlock."

An indeterminate time later, he awoke flat on his back in a room on the third floor of Raven's Reach manor.

FOUR

THE ONE OTHER PERSON WHO never responded to the invitation was a man named Jacob Martinelli. He was thirty-nine years old but looked at least a decade older thanks to many years of hard living. Jake worked part-time as a bagger at the supermarket down the street from where he lived. It was a shit job, but given his spotty work history and well-known reputation for unreliability, it was the best he could do. The rest of his income was derived from patrolling the grimy streets of his shitty neighborhood with a stolen grocery cart he used for collecting things to recycle. He devoted nearly as many hours to that as to his actual job. Took a lot of empty cans and bottles to add up to much.

At the end of each week, he was lucky if he had more than a few coins to rub together. Most of the money that didn't go toward paying his weekly rent at the dumpy motel he called home was spent on cheap liquor. It wasn't physically possible for him to get through the day without booze. If he didn't maintain his regular intake, he'd get the shakes and a miserable, pounding headache that wouldn't go away until he was able to drink again. Even at the supermarket he often had to sneak away to take quick maintenance sips of vodka from the flask he kept in his back pocket. Most of his co-workers knew what he was doing, but they didn't give him guff about it because he was never gone for more than a couple minutes. Also, most of them were dedicated potheads who were always puffing away out back at break time. This included most of the supervisors. Giving him shit over his maintenance nips would've made them hypocrites.

Besides, they all remembered the time he'd had a seizure at the front end of the store, which happened on a day when he'd forgotten to fill his flask before reporting to work. No one wanted to see that happen again. It was horrifying. As long as he didn't get noticeably loaded or slur his words when talking to customers, allowing him to indulge his addiction seemed a fair price to pay if it helped prevent any similar incidents from occurring in the future.

Jake had a hard life and he was never particularly happy, but he'd worked out a system for dealing with his dismal existence as best he could. As long as it wasn't disrupted, he figured he could go on trudging through the days for at least another decade, maybe a little longer. By then he'd be old and broken down and what would any of it matter anyway? A few kind souls had tried suggesting another way for him. Some time in a detox center, possibly, followed by daily AA meetings for the rest of his life. He was told to imagine how good he would feel if he could get free of his addiction and work on improving his overall health. They meant well, but Jake wasn't interested. He knew what they said was possible if he put in the effort, but he didn't want that better life. It wasn't meant for the likes of him. He didn't deserve it. All he wanted was the oblivion of booze. There were things a prolonged period of sobriety would help him remember. Bad things that should remain submerged.

Bad things from a long time ago.

In late November, he was sent home early from his supermarket shift one day because it was dead at the store. This was fine with him. He was only losing an hour's pay and now he'd be able to commence his serious night drinking a little earlier than usual. His first stop on the way home was the liquor store, where he loaded up on Popov vodka and grabbed two bottles of Boone's Farm apple wine as a special treat. The Boone's Farm was a bit of a splurge, but he wanted to get extra drunk—even for him—and hopefully sleep through the night better than he usually did. If he could do that, he might not remember the bad dreams about those long-ago bad things.

When he got back to the weekly motel, he checked his mailbox and found the invitation waiting for him. Not knowing what it was yet, he paid it little mind as he went up to his second-floor room and set about preparing an ice-filled pitcher of vodka mixed with cranberry juice. He sat at the table in the little kitchenette area of his room and downed two glasses of this mixture before reaching for the envelope from Raven's Reach.

He tore it open and pulled out the folded piece of heavy card stock. First thing he noticed was how fancy it was with the cursive script.

He read the invitation

Then he read it again.

Checking the envelope again, he found the accompanying note with further instructions and the check. The check was for five grand. Jake hadn't seen that much money at one time since he was in his twenties, back when he was still maintaining a semi-respectable life in mainstream society. Back when he was still able to hold the bad memories at bay without drinking himself into a daily stupor. Among other things, the invitation said he'd be sent a plane ticket for the trip to Raven's Reach as soon as he called the number to RSVP. Paid airfare struck Jake as an extreme extravagance on top of the big check. He couldn't imagine why anyone would arrange travel for a piece of shit like himself unless they had some sinister ulterior motive.

He focused on the date of the mysterious event.

Fucking Christmas Day. Same day as . . .

Something flickered inside his head.

Images from long ago.

Jake dropped the invitation from his shaking hands and abruptly stood up, the chair skidding away from him across the kitchenette's scuffed and dingy linoleum floor. A shuddery breath escaped his lips. His brow was suddenly wet with sweat. After taking some moments to steady himself as best he could, he grabbed one of the bottles of Boone's Farm from the fridge, opened it, and drank deeply, downing more than a third of it in one long pull. He paused to take a few big breaths and then he guzzled down more cheap wine. This process continued until the bottle was empty. Barely more than two minutes had passed since he'd screwed off the cap. He tossed the bottle across the room and it shattered when it struck the wall. Someone in the next room made a muffled noise of protest.

The rapid influx of booze wasn't nearly enough to calm the raging storm inside him. There was no way he could drink enough to escape the truth. Not this time. The past was reaching out to him in the form of that hateful invitation. That date. He knew it was connected. No way could it be a coincidence.

INVITATION TO DEATH

Jacob Martinelli was a nobody to those who knew him now. Worthless. A zero. A wreck of a human being for whom one could only feel pity. Or, sometimes, especially on those occasions when he passed out in a public place, a deep revulsion. He'd been kicked and spat on more times than he could ever count.

He was a walking casualty.

But he wasn't completely without power, not even now. He still had some small level of personal agency remaining. Control over his destiny. Jake decided he would have nothing to do with whatever was happening at Raven's Reach on Christmas Day.

Nothing to do with the hurtful past ever again.

He grabbed the other bottle of Boone's from the fridge and drank it down, albeit at a slightly slower rate than before. By the time he reached the bottom of the second bottle, an unexpected calm had come over him. He realized he was tired of working so hard to hide from those old ghosts. They didn't need to keep haunting and tormenting him anymore.

Jake set the empty bottle on the table and walked out of his room, leaving the door open. As he walked down the hallway to the stairs, he passed acquaintances who nodded perfunctory greetings. They didn't really care about him and he sure as hell didn't care about them.

Outside it was raining and cold. He shivered as he stepped to the street corner and waited for the right moment. The light at the intersection cycled through a few times as he waited, cars and trucks whizzing by at inappropriately high speeds for a couple minutes every time the light turned green again. After about the fifth time, the right candidate finally came along. He stepped out in front of the speeding city bus and was flattened in the street. Multiple sets of heavy wheels rolled over him before alarmed motorists could come to a screeching halt.

Several people got out of their cars to check on him.

But it was too late.

Bradley Winthorpe's high school best friend was dead.

FIVE

A BLACK MERCEDES SUV ARRIVED at the gate to the private mountain road more than thirty minutes ahead of schedule. The man driving the SUV was George Barrington. He tried entering the access code they'd been given three times before a voice issuing from a speaker informed them the code would not work until the designated time.

"That's such bullshit. We're already here. What's the point of waiting? Open the fucking gate. Pretty please."

There was a pause.

Then the voice spoke again. "The code will expire after two more premature entries. Move your vehicle away from the gate and wait for the designated time."

Barrington gaped at the speaker, shaking his head in disbelief. "You've gotta be fucking kidding me."

This time there was no response at all.

Colette Hammerschmidt sighed and shifted slightly in the front passenger seat. "We clearly have no choice but to abide by their rules, George. Move us away from the damn gate."

Barrington shook his head again and muttered under his breath. "Unbelievable."

Despite his obvious agitation, he didn't hesitate to do as she said. The road leading out here from Thornton dead-ended at a point slightly beyond the turnoff to the gate. There was a largish open area where one could turn around and head back toward town. Barrington steered the SUV into this area and got it turned about so it was facing the access gate from a distance of about fifteen yards. He scowled and grumbled unintelligibly for a moment before popping a stick of gum in his mouth and chewing aggressively. The gum was an oral substitute meant to wean him off smoking cigarettes. The constant desire for a cigarette was making him miserable, but he would not surrender to the urge. Not today and not ever.

Colette knew this because the no smoking mandate was her doing. She'd made it clear she would not marry the man unless he was smoke-free for a period of at least a full year. In truth, she had no intention of marrying him even then, but that wasn't something he needed to know just yet. It wasn't anything she needed to think about too seriously right now. She had another six months before she would have to break the news to him, which she would do in the presence of bodyguards. George could be a bit volatile at times. She doubted he'd try to hurt her, but one could never be too cautious in such matters.

George came from a quality family. Good bloodlines. Old money. He was the kind of man who should have been set for life without ever raising a sweat or doing an honest day's work. But there was a monkey in the wrench in the form of some long-standing and bitter dispute with his father, the nature of which George was perpetually reluctant to discuss. He was ultimately disinherited and had his generous monthly allowance cut off shortly after his thirtieth birthday. Because he had no talents or business acumen of his own, he found himself desperate within a short period of time.

That was where Colette stepped in.

She had money aplenty. Millions and millions. Much of it was money earned by her late husband before his death. More of it came from selling his business shortly after he was put in the ground. The sale was made on the stipulation that she hold onto a certain amount of stock and remain on the board of directors. The business was doing well. Better than ever, in fact. More money was coming in all the time. She definitely had no need of the ten million dollars she stood to earn for spending the evening at Raven's Reach, but that wasn't the point.

The point was she enjoyed the current power dynamic that existed between them. She'd agreed to split the sum with George once the money was wired to her bank after their stay at Raven's Reach. This was another promise she had no intention of keeping. Despite her taking care of him for the last year, her would-be second husband oozed desperation from his every pore. He wanted nothing more than to get his hands on some solid funds of his own and not be completely dependent on someone else for once in his life. The yearning for this consumed him.

The anticipation of seeing his face drop when she eventually announced he would not be getting any of the money—not even a small token—was an exciting thing. Even then, despite his inevitable anger, he would be dependent on her and would have no choice but to continue kissing her ass and occasionally groveling before her. As they sat there and stared at the access gate, she wondered what he might do once he was finally and fully banished from her life. Perhaps he would kill himself. How thrilling that would be, to drive a man to suicide. A very different experience from killing a man and successfully passing it off as suicide, a thing she'd already accomplished, but one bound to be almost as gratifying.

But, no, George almost certainly wouldn't take his own life.

He would be furious and even more desperate than ever for a time, but that quality breeding would almost certainly save him once again. He was incredibly handsome and still fairly young at thirty-one. It wouldn't be long before he attracted the attention of another sugar mama, possibly even one with a kinder nature than her own. All that aside, George was far too narcissistic for suicide. In his view, nothing in this world was more important than his well-being. He would laugh heartily at even the mere suggestion of self-harm.

She sighed, thinking about it.

It was really too bad.

She wanted to ruin him for the simple sport of it, but sometimes even a very rich woman couldn't get *everything* she wanted.

They'd been waiting there at the end of the road for about ten minutes when they first heard the faint rumble of another vehicle's engine, a noise that steadily increased over the next several seconds. Colette craned her head around and soon saw a red SUV coming up the road toward them. The vehicle's headlights came on as it approached, blotchy globes of bright light floating in the deepening gloom. A misting cold rain mixed with tiny snowflakes made it difficult to tell how many people were in the red SUV almost until it pulled up at the gate.

By then Colette could see there were two adults sitting up front. Their faces were a blur through the rain-speckled windows, but she had the sense the two up front were in early middle age. Late thirties, perhaps. Around her own age. A man and woman. A couple, undoubtedly, and probably a married one. This she deduced from the slightly smaller forms in the middle seats. The couple's teenaged offspring, no doubt, a deduction that made her mouth curl in distaste.

Colette despised children and preferred to avoid them whenever possible. It was this attitude that led to some of her bitterest conflicts with her late husband. David had wanted kids. A real family. Whereas Colette only wanted to play and have fun. She reveled in the socialite life and had zero interest in giving that up to raise squalling brats. Sure, she could have hired a nanny to handle the ugliest aspects of child-rearing, such as changing diapers and cleaning up various gross messes, but even then their mere existence would still create too many drains on her time. She also had no desire to go through the messiness of childbirth. As far as she was concerned, the whole idea was a complete non-starter, but David was persistent. After years of trying and failing to convince her regarding the supposed joys of parenthood, he shifted tactics and suggested they start thinking about finding some kids to adopt.

That was when she decided David Hammerschmidt had to die.

George abruptly spat his gum out the open window on his side. "Here we go."

The driver of the red SUV had just leaned out through his window to enter his admittance code, and now the long bar gate was swinging open. George changed gears and quickly drove the Mercedes into position behind the other vehicle, which they could now see was an older model Kia. One of those irritating family stick figure decals was affixed to the lower right corner of the back window. It was so odd, really. Colette would not have guessed anyone attending an exclusive event for rich elites would be driving anything like an old Kia, a vehicle for commoners.

"What are you doing, George?"

He grunted. "Isn't it obvious? The gate's opening. I'll just slide in behind these suburban losers before it can close again."

Colette sighed wearily. "The gate is opening because these people have arrived at their designated time. Obviously the people staging whatever this event is have assigned staggered arrival times. For what reason I do not know, but we will respect their schedule. Back up again. We will enter at our proper time."

George shook his head. "No."

She was staring straight ahead as he said this, still transfixed by the annoying decal. It stirred a strange sense of revulsion deep inside her, possibly because it was a reminder of her former life with David. A symbol of the life he'd wanted. The one she'd opted to deny him forever.

Then the defiant utterance of her current beau registered.

Her head swiveled slowly toward him, bulging eyes radiating malevolence and indignation. "What did you say?"

He looked at her and sneered. "You heard me. I'm tired of being bossed around by you. We're going in now."

Her hands curled into fists as she turned fully toward him, heart thudding rapidly in the face of this unprecedented insolence. "You're forgetting your place. Back up this instant, or when we arrive I will have the man or lady of the house summon a cab to take you to the nearest airport."

George snorted. "Like fuck you will."

His right hand came away from the steering wheel and cracked hard across her face. A searing flash of pain made her cry out as she shrank away from him, tears springing instantly to her eyes. George hit the gas and the Mercedes roared through before the gate could swing back into place.

George laughed. "There. You see? We're in. No more waiting around like second-class citizens. No big fuckin' deal."

Colette was as far away from him as she could get and still be inside the vehicle, with her back up against the door. She stared at him silently through wide eyes still leaking tears, looking at him now as if she'd never truly seen him before. Not for what he really was. His veneer of submissiveness was gone, vanished without a trace. This thing sitting behind the wheel of her Mercedes might as well have been an alien creature.

He smirked. "You look scared. Good. Things are gonna be different from now on, bitch. I'm done letting you treat me like an amusing toy, of making me feel like less than a man. From now on, I'm in charge. And don't think you can just cut me out of your life when we get home. I'll be keeping a close watch on you at all times. I get even the slightest hint of you trying some shit like that, I'll fuckin' kill you. You hear me?"

Colette sniffled. She said nothing.

George raised a fist and waved it at her, his face a twisted mask of rage as he roared at her. "*I said, do you fucking hear me!?*"

Until then she'd never had occasion to notice how huge his closed fist looked, especially up close like this. It looked like a battering ram made of flesh and bulging veins. She swallowed hard and made herself nod. "I hear you."

He laughed as his hand returned to the steering wheel. "I like you better like this. Crying and shaking like a frightened little animal." He grabbed his crotch and squeezed it. "It's getting me all riled up. Think I'm gonna fuck you extra hard tonight. Have you face-down on the fucking bed while I take you up the ass for once. How's that sound?"

Colette said nothing as she wiped away her tears.

George was both right and wrong at the same time.

Things had changed between them now. Suddenly. Permanently. There could never be any going back to the way things were just minutes ago.

He was right about that.

But he was wrong about her lack of say in the matter. He would *not* be in charge of her life from this point forward. Nor would he violently have his way with her in bed tonight. This was sheer delusion on his part, common sense overridden by blind machismo. Not only would she cut him out of her own life, but she had every intention of removing him from life on earth entirely before their time on this mountain was over.

SIX

AS THE GATE STARTED TO swing open, Alan Dozier happened to glance at his rearview mirror at what he immediately recognized as the exact wrong moment. Glancing up even a second or two earlier would've spared him a massive amount of inner turmoil, because he would've missed the shocking thing that happened in the vehicle behind him. A guy who looked like a movie star sat behind the wheel of an SUV that looked several times more expensive than Sandra's old Kia. He had wavy blond hair and a chiseled chin. The woman in the passenger seat was clearly several years older than him at least, but she was an attractive lady in her own right, very cultured and elegant-looking.

They appeared to be arguing about something, which in itself was not an alarming thing. People—couples especially—argued all the time. He and Sandra had a mostly calm relationship compared to many of their friends and neighbors, but even they had the occasional doozy of a disagreement now and then. It was inevitable over the course of any long-term relationship. In all their time together, however, not once had those disagreements ever turned physically violent, which was why it was startling to see the ridiculously handsome man suddenly backhand his female companion.

He gasped.

His hands tightened around the steering wheel and his foot

mashed down on the gas pedal, causing the Kia to shoot forward at a speed inadvisable on a road as narrow and precarious as this one. He eased off the gas and had the vehicle under control again within seconds, but the damage was done.

After making a startled noise of her own, Sandra looked up from her phone and glanced at him. "Jesus, Alan. Are you all right?"

Alan heaved a big breath and shook his head. Then he summoned a big smile he hoped didn't look too obviously false and briefly met her gaze. "No, honey. I'm fine. Had myself a little brain fart, that's all." He cleared his throat and swiftly changed the subject. "I wonder how far up the mountain this mansion is? Elevation's already making my ears pop."

Sandra shrugged. "I looked up what I could about Raven's Reach online, but there's not a lot out there, not even on the town's website. A little strange considering it's such a massive old estate. You'd think it'd be, like, really historically significant. A major local attraction kind of deal."

Alan nodded. "Yeah, that is weird. Thornton's even named after the guy who originally had the place built, isn't it?"

At that point, Sandra launched into a full recap of everything she'd learned about Raven's Reach while researching the place online. Despite her complaints regarding the dearth of authoritative sources, telling all she knew required several minutes.

While she talked, her words faded to a drone in Alan's head as his attention returned to the rearview mirror. The black SUV had slipped behind them a bit after that quick burst of speed, but it was closer again now. The man sneered as he spoke to the woman in a clearly agitated way. Even angry, he still looked like a goddamn movie star. Alan already disliked the guy because of what he'd done, but his looks added an extra dimension to his irritation. The reason why wasn't a mystery. The guy reminded him a little too much of popular, good-looking jerks who'd pushed him around in high school. Guys who'd beaten him up more than once.

The woman's face was tear-streaked, her makeup ruined. She'd pushed herself up against the door, as far away from her asshole companion as she could get without exiting the vehicle. The road was rising steeply upward and any leap from the SUV's passenger side at this point would mean a probably fatal tumble from an already considerable height. Alan watched the woman repeatedly cringe as the man continued barking undoubtedly vile things at her. He hoped she wouldn't choose to throw herself from the vehicle out of sheer desperation or hopelessness.

He felt bad for her and despised the man for what he'd done, but the situation also made him uptight and uncomfortable. The old-fashioned part of him that believed strongly in some level of chivalry felt it was his duty as a man to intervene and prevent any further harm to the woman. No doubt that would be the honorable thing to do. It might even function as a good object lesson for his son and daughter. Show the boy that you can't stand for that kind of thing. Show the daughter that some men would still do the right thing when the moment called for it.

On the other hand . . .

Good intentions were fine in theory, but sometimes in the real world they could get you in trouble. Or hurt. What he could see of the man was enough to suggest he had a muscular build and was probably a good bit taller than he was. Alan tried to imagine himself getting up in the guy's face and admonishing or threatening him for what he'd done. He hated it, but this was impossible to envision in a way that wasn't laughable. At best, he'd get laughed at and shoved out of the way. At worst, he'd get knocked down and have his face rubbed in the dirt, just like the bullies used to do back in high school. The thought of his kids witnessing something like that happening to him was just intolerable.

And yet, he couldn't just do nothing. His conscience wouldn't allow that. Perhaps once they were settled inside the manor, he could seek out someone in charge and pull them aside for a little chat. By passing on knowledge of what he'd seen, responsibility for it wouldn't all be on him. He let out a big breath as this thought came to him, feeling slightly relieved. Still, he kept his gaze partly on the rearview mirror the rest of the way up the mountain road. Although things obviously remained tense between the couple in the black SUV, he did not see the man strike the woman again. A good thing, because if it *had* happened again, he would be left with no choice but to attempt intervention despite his misgivings.

As he took the Kia around another swooping bend in the road, he saw the end of it a short way ahead and got his first glimpse of the manor, which was even more imposingly huge than he'd imagined. He heard his kids gasp in the back and sensed the way they suddenly leaned forward, captivated by the wonder of what they were seeing.

Alan remembered scoffing when they received the invitation to the event at Raven's Reach. The Doziers were an unassuming middle-class family of no particular note. He loved his wife and kids to pieces and to him nobody else in the world could compare, but he knew their place in the scheme of things. They were like a million other regular families. He and Sandra both had good, stable jobs. They made a decent enough living that they lived in relative comfort and didn't want for too much. Sure, they went without things now and then, but that was no big deal. You worked hard and made do with what you had. It was the American way.

So why would some mysterious wealthy person send them an apparently real check for fifty thousand dollars as enticement to attending an unspecified event at which they could supposedly earn an additional million dollars? He'd thought about it and thought about it, but he'd come up with no explanation that made sense to him.

The prospect of all that money excited him, of course, even in the midst of his skepticism and concern. That fifty grand wasn't much less than what he and Sandra made in a single year combined. And a million damn dollars? Heck, that seemed like almost all the money in the world. So much money it was like something out of an impossible fantasy. But then the check cleared and at that point there was no chance they wouldn't try for the whole million bucks. He and Sandra both knew they'd never get a chance at that much money again.

They had to go for it.

And now here they were.

Alan slowed down as he pulled up outside the wide-open gate to the huge property. He stared up at the massive manor, feeling awe wash over him as he shook his head in wonder. Even against the darkening sky, the size and sprawl of the thing was incredible to behold.

It was a nice moment.

Then the asshole in the black SUV laid on his horn for an extended moment, a jarring intrusion that made Alan scowl as he glanced again at his rearview mirror.

His son, Tommy, turned around in his seat and stared at the vehicle behind them. "What's that guy's problem?"

Good question, kid, Alan thought, shaking his head. *Dear God, please don't let that son of a bitch ruin our night.*

He hit the gas and drove through the gate.

SEVEN

IN A ROOM IN THE manor's western wing, a woman began to stir from a deep slumber. The only faint illumination was courtesy of the room's one window, which overlooked a garden and the lush surrounding grounds to the rear of the property. That faint light was fading moment by moment as the last remaining traces of sunlight continued to drain from the sky.

Alexandra Harcourt's eyes fluttered open just in time for her to roll toward the window and gauge the approximate time of day. She knew the sky looked like this at a certain hour of both the morning and evening, but within seconds she knew this must be the latter, because even within that short time the world beyond the barrier of glass seemed to darken perceptibly.

That much was easy enough to determine, but other aspects of her current situation were slightly slower coming into focus. Soon, however, she realized something wasn't quite right about the mattress beneath her slender body. She shifted slightly in the bed and the nature of that "not quite right" aspect came to her. *This* mattress was softer and more comfortable by far than the one she slept in nearly every night at home. She lifted her head off the pillow and squinted in the rapidly fading light, making out just enough of her surroundings to confirm she *wasn't* in her home.

Beyond the unfamiliar feel of the mattress, the size of the room's lone window was the most obvious clue. Even with the curtains drawn partially shut, this window was clearly several times larger than the one in the bedroom of her apartment. Not only that, but the space between the edge of the mattress and the window was significant. Her entire bedroom, with all its secondhand furniture and clutter, would easily fit in that space. The bed itself was more than twice the size of her own queen-sized bed. All of this added up to an overall impression of being in an absolutely *huge* room, the kind she couldn't imagine existing outside of an extremely wealthy person's mansion.

All these things struck her as strange but only mildly upsetting at first, mostly because she still wasn't quite all the way back to full wakefulness. She felt drugged. Several minutes passed before her brain started functioning at a normal level, but at last it did and only then did a sense of real terror begin to overtake her.

She sat up and swept a plush blanket away from her naked body. Hurriedly scrabbling toward the edge of the bed, she eased herself over the side and felt her bare feet touch a cold hardwood floor. The floors of her apartment were all carpeted, save for the cheap linoleum in the kitchen. Not that she needed any additional evidence of where she wasn't at that point, but the stark difference cemented the reality of the mysterious change in location and sent her terror level skyrocketing even higher.

Now that she was on her feet, she became aware of a hitherto unnoticed heaviness encircling her left wrist. Some object. One not just heavy, but *cold*. She clutched at it with her right hand and found a bracelet of steel encircling the wrist. Something even heavier was attached to the bracelet. She shook her hand and heard a rattle of chain links.

Oh, fuck!

She noticed a dark shape at the side of the bed and made her way toward it. Feeling around in the dark, her hand found the surface of a large night table. With some more feeling around, she found the base of a lamp. Her hand moved along the curved column extending upward from the base until she found a switch, which she promptly snapped on. Light muted by the heavy shade covering the bulb drove back some of the darkness. Fear that some pervert was in the room with her, perhaps watching from a dark corner, made her spin about in search of the theoretical creep.

No one was in the room with her, at least not that she could see. A tall wardrobe stood against the wall opposite the foot of the bed, its doors closed. She supposed it was possible someone might be lurking inside the thing. Or perhaps even under the bed, perhaps within grabbing range of her ankles. She shrieked again and quickly backed several feet away from the bed before dropping to her hands and knees, breathing hard as her eyes scanned the space beneath and found nothing.

Sighing in at least temporary relief, her attention returned to the cuff around her left wrist. The chain extending away from it was of generous length and was partly coiled on the floor, with the other end attached to a metal plate fastened to the wall between the edge of the bed and the night table. She spent the next several moments testing its length and found she was able to move about the greater part of the room with relative ease.

She went to the window, which she quickly determined would be impossible to open without finding some heavy object with which she could smash through it. She instantly recognized several reasons why this would be a waste of time and effort. Firstly, the glass looked significantly thicker than the usual window pane. Smashing through it would not be easy, even with the aid of, say, a heavy cinder block, which she didn't happen to have handy anyway. Also, the window appeared to be three stories off the ground. While long, the chain would not extend nearly that far. Not that she'd be stupid enough to attempt escape without first freeing herself of the damn chain.

Now, *if* she could get free of the chain, remove it from the wall, and anchor it to something nearer the window, perhaps she could, in theory, lower herself to the ground . . . or at least close enough to let go of it and fall the rest of the way with a reasonable assurance of safety. One thing for sure, she would not be able to jump or drop safely from the window. It was too far and she was in no hurry to mangle herself.

The only way she could reach the door to the room was by crawling back over the mattress in order to approach it in a straight line. It would not reach if she went around the end of the bed, a thing she determined by trying it both ways. When she did reach the door, she tried the old-fashioned knob and was unsurprised to find it would not budge. She rattled it fiercely anyway and muttered several frustrated curses. There was no obvious way to unlock it from the inside. An impulse to bang on the door with her fist and call out for help came and went. She was in no hurry to attract the attention of whoever had brought her to this place. Not yet anyway.

Stuck for any obvious way out of her dilemma for the time being, Alexandra returned to the bed and sat on the edge facing the maddeningly immovable door. The lock did not appear to be of a complicated type, judging from the old-fashioned knob and plate. It was possible a more thorough search of the room might turn up a bobby pin or some similar object she could easily insert in the keyhole. She imagined she could then flip the lock mechanism with relative ease. Not that it really mattered. Even if she could open the door, the taut chain would prevent her from venturing any farther than the edge of the hallway she assumed was outside the room.

Her thoughts thus turned to the mystery of who might have abducted her. In her younger days, like so many other women, she'd had the occasional bit of trouble with young men who desired her but wouldn't leave her alone despite being firmly brushed off multiple times. One of these men was so creepily persistent she wound up having to get a restraining order against him, which he proceeded to violate multiple times until he was finally arrested. He was only in jail a day or two, but the arrest must have scared him, because after that she never heard from the guy again. His name was Stephen Bain. She didn't think this could be his doing because she'd kept tabs on him for several years after the arrest, a habit born of understandable paranoia, but one she'd finally let go of a few years ago. The last she knew he was happily married, and he and his wife lived in a nice house in the suburbs with their young daughter. She didn't doubt he was likely still a creep on some hidden level—she didn't believe men like that ever fully changed—but her trouble with him was more than a decade in the past. Clearly he'd moved on.

No, this was the work of some unknown other person, possibly a co-worker or some male friend who'd successfully hidden a darker side. Her creep radar was pretty good by now and for years she'd managed to steer clear of friendly relationships with men who seemed off or dangerous in any way. She guessed it was possible one of her friendly male acquaintances had fooled her into believing they were safe when actually they weren't, but even if that were true, she didn't really buy it as a viable explanation for her current situation.

The only thing she knew for an absolute fact—or could deduce with a high level of certainty—was that someone had drugged her and taken her to this place. She'd been kidnapped. Not technically against her will, she supposed, because she hadn't been conscious at the time, but that was semantics. If she'd had any say in the matter, she wouldn't be in this strange place, stripped naked with her wrist chained to the wall. She'd gone to bed in her underwear and a t-shirt. At some point, either back at her apartment or after her arrival here, her abductor had removed those garments. She couldn't imagine a non-ominous reason for that and feared she'd been molested during her period of unconsciousness.

Thinking about that possibility, she whimpered softly and started trembling at the edge of the bed. She was soon distracted from these disturbing thoughts, however, by a noise out in the hallway she hadn't glimpsed yet. She heard a faint rattle and squeak and, in another moment, she guessed something on wheels—a cart, possibly—was being slowly pushed down the hallway. The cart—or whatever it was—was getting steadily closer. Then, abruptly, the rattling sound came to a stop right outside the door.

A silent moment passed.

Then she started trembling harder and crossed her arms over her breasts when she heard the sound of a key rattling in the lock. She sat on the bed and shielded her nakedness the best she could. A distinct click followed and in the next moment a tall, lanky man dressed all in black wheeled a cart into the room. Resting inside the tray-like gray surface of the cart was an old TV, the boxy kind that had been obsolete for decades. Trailing from the back of the set was a power cord and a coiled coaxial cable. Alexandra couldn't see the tall man's face because he wore a black hood over his head with slits cut in the front for eyeholes. She saw the man's blue eyes dart briefly in her direction once before flicking away. He said nothing as he wheeled the cart over to the large wardrobe, where he went to work connecting cord and cable to wall outlets.

Alexandra studied the man closely while he worked, trying to tell whether anything about him reminded her of anyone she knew, soon deducing the answer was no. She couldn't think of anyone in either her work or personal life who was built quite like this man was, which made her wonder if she'd been abducted by an obsessed stranger. A sex pervert, possibly, who meant to keep her until he was tired of her. Or dead.

Probably the latter.

She whimpered again as a heartbreaking reality came crashing down on her.

I'm never getting out of here.

The man in the hood stood up. He turned on the TV and turned the channel selector over a few notches, leaving it tuned to a screen filled with white static. That done, he headed silently back toward the door, this time not glancing her way even once.

"Stop!"

Alexandra impulsively called out to him just as he was about to step out into the hallway. She was terrified of interacting with who-ever this was, but she found herself consumed with a desperate need to know more about her situation. She didn't know what this man had planned. This might be her last chance to learn anything for a while.

"Who are you? Why did you take me?"

He made a sound somewhere between a sigh and a grumble. "I didn't take you. Keep the TV on."

She got up from the bed and tremblingly took a few steps in his direction, her eyes filling with tears as she said, "Please let me go. I . . . I'll do anything. Whatever you want, just please let me go."

The man said nothing.

He stepped out into the hallway and closed the door. A moment later the key rattled in the lock, a sound followed again by that distinct click. The sound of his footsteps slowly receded as he walked away. Alexandra spent some moments feeling numb as she stared at the closed door. Soon, however, her legs turned rubbery and she dropped despairingly to her knees, covering her face with her hands as she began to weep uncontrollably.

Never getting out of here.

Never, never, never . . .

EIGHT

ONCE SHE AND GEORGE WERE up in their spacious room in the eastern wing of Raven's Reach manor, Colette Hammerschmidt's first priority was to find the bathroom and close herself inside it for a while. She remained consumed with a mixture of fury and terror at what George had done to her and was desperate for some time away from him.

The current circumstances, however, meant she couldn't get nearly as far away as she wanted. For the time being, they were stuck with this close quarters situation, but the barrier of a bathroom door would be better than nothing. It would give her time to breathe and think, to figure out a way of separating herself from the smirking brute without having to kill him immediately. After that initial white-heat flash of murderous rage, she'd concluded murdering him at Raven's Reach would be too potentially messy, too rife with the possibility of self-implication. He would die. Of that there was no doubt. But she would need to wait until she returned home and could discreetly engage the services of a professional killer.

The only problem was the room did not appear to have an easily accessible adjacent bathroom. The only door was the one going in and out of the room, unless one counted the doors to the massive wardrobe standing opposite the foot of the canopied bed. She strongly suspected a magical gateway to fucking Narnia did not lurk behind those doors. On the off-chance she was wrong about that, she dropped her travel bag at the foot of the bed and went straight to the wardrobe, pulling it open. No Narnia. Too bad. That fantastical god-damn wonderland would have come with its own set of complications and hazards, but in light of her current feelings about George, she wouldn't have hesitated to step through the portal had it actually been there.

Inside the wardrobe was a selection of elegant-looking designer dresses that looked like they would probably fit her. Highly expensive ones, too. She had a hunch this was by design and that these were not garments left behind by some other woman. There were no men's clothes hanging in the wardrobe. Of course not. George was an afterthought. Her worthless plus one that she now wished to subtract from her life.

Colette closed the wardrobe and headed for the door to their room.

George hurriedly put himself in her path, putting his back against the door and spreading his arms. "Where do you think you're going?"

Colette needed every ounce of willpower she possessed to keep from verbally lashing out at him in her usual way. She was in no hurry to experience the crack of that backhand across her face again. "There's no bathroom in here. I need to pee and freshen up."

George shook his head. "You heard that Lurch-looking motherfucker." He was referring to the lanky individual with the livid facial scar who'd prevented them from entering the grounds of the estate ahead of the scheduled time. This was after appearing from seemingly out of nowhere. The tall weirdo allowed the family in the Kia to pass through and enter the manor, but made George and herself wait an additional twenty minutes. George was not happy, to say the least, but the strange man had a deeply unsettling vibe about him, easily intimidating him into temporary silence. "We're to stay in our room until summoned. If we don't, we forfeit the prize. I'm not about to let that happen."

Colette frowned. "But I have to pee." She really did, actually, now that she was thinking about it. The urge was quite strong, in fact. "What am I supposed to do?"

George shrugged.

He looked away from her and slowly cast his gaze about the room. His expression changed after a few seconds, displaying deep amusement. He pointed to something she guessed was in the general vicinity of the bed. "I think we're meant to use that."

She sighed and turned away from him, following the direction of his pointing finger. Beneath the little table next to the bed was a large ceramic chamber pot. "Oh, for fuck's sake."

George chuckled.

She looked at him, trying out a beseeching tone as she said, "I can't actually be expected to urinate into that thing. This isn't the fucking 1800s."

He laughed. "You sure about that?" He waved a hand in the air. "Because, I mean . . . take a look around. This place is like something out of one of those gothic dramas you like to watch on fucking PBS. Maybe we passed through a time tunnel or something when we went through that gate."

Colette rolled her eyes. "Nice theory. But I'd say the electric lights and old-timey TV kind of disprove it."

George shrugged. "Maybe so. Fact remains, you're not leaving the room until we get the go-ahead. You gotta go bad enough, use the fucking chamber pot. Unless you'd rather just go on the floor."

Colette made a sound of frustration and stamped a foot. As soon as she did this, she flinched inwardly, fearing George would take it as sufficient excuse to smack her upside the head again. His jawline did tighten perceptibly, indicating a possibly imminent explosion of anger, but she sought to defuse it by spinning quickly away from him. She retrieved the chamber pot from its place under the night table and looked at him. "You mind turning around so I can at least have some privacy while I pee?"

The look on George's face hardened, suggesting he didn't give one single damn about her privacy or personal boundaries. "Turn my back on you after the day we've had? I don't think so, bitch." He chuckled and waggled an eyebrow at her in a way that made her skin crawl. "Like I said already, you gotta go bad enough, you know what to do, but I'm gonna watch while you do it." He smirked and grabbed his crotch. "Shit, that might even be kind of hot."

Colette glared at him a moment.

Then she shook her head. "Forget it. I'll just hold it. It won't be fun, but I can manage until they let us leave the goddamn room."

George cracked his knuckles as he took a menacing step toward her. "Piss in the goddamn pot."

His tone promised pain and a lot of it if she didn't comply. There was no real choice here. No option that wasn't demeaning or dangerous. Fuming inwardly, she slapped the pot down on the hard-wood floor, lowered her panties, lifted the hem of her dress, and squatted over the thing. Colette rarely ever felt self-conscious about anything, but this was different. The leering, nauseating way George was watching her made her guts feel like a nest of squirming snakes. As a result, she was unable to go right away, despite the urgency of the need. She had to close her eyes and take several deep breaths to get sufficiently relaxed. In another moment, she heard her stream pattering into the previously empty pot. She felt more disgust when she opened her eyes and saw George massaging his hugely erect cock through the tented front of his slacks. He really was a gross human being in practically every way imaginable.

She looked away from him and in another few moments her stream slowed to a trickle and finally stopped. Glancing around, she saw nothing with which she could wipe herself, nor was there a sink in the room in which she could wash her hands. More insults to basic decency. She pulled up her panties and returned the pot to its place under the night table.

Before she could do anything else, George came at her in a rush, roughly grabbed hold of her, and pushed her face-down onto the bed. She cried out in startled surprise as he fell atop her and thrust his erection against her ass. She squealed and yelled at him to get off of her, but he only laughed in her ear and continued grinding against her.

"Told you what I was gonna do once I got you up here," he said, grunting and snuffling like a pig in a trough. "Didn't believe me, huh?" He laughed in his oily way as he slid a hand beneath her and pawed at her breasts. "Gonna go up your ass just like I said. Up your cunt, too, and maybe finish by making you choke on my cock. I bet you'd love that."

He got up on his knees and started tugging at the zipper of his slacks, still straddling her in a way that prevented her from moving around easily. There was, however, just enough extra space between their bodies now that she could lift herself up slightly. He laughed, taking this as extra encouragement, as sexual positioning. As if he'd overwhelmed her with his raw animal sexuality, making her a slave to mindless lust.

Glancing over her shoulder, Colette saw they were relatively close to the edge of the bed. Bracing her hands against the mattress, she shoved herself backward with all the strength she could muster, which, as it turned out, was plenty enough to do the job. George cried out as he toppled backward off the bed, crashing hard to the floor.

Colette scrambled around and dropped to the floor. She grabbed the chamber pot, hearing her piss slosh around inside it as she hurriedly swung it around. The pot crashed against the side of George's head just as he was starting to sit up, immediately causing him to flop onto his back again. Before he could make another attempt to get up, she dropped to her knees at his side, raised the pot high over her head, and brought it down with all her might. This time the blow was delivered with enough force to cause the ceramic pot to shatter in her hands. She let the pieces fall away as she sat there panting for several moments, watching in amazed wonder as a rapidly spreading pool of blood formed around George Barrington's head. Some more minutes passed, during which her brain was in a numb state of shock. Nothing resembling coherent thought occurred during those minutes.

Shortly thereafter, panic set in.

I had to do it, she thought. *It was self-defense.*

People will know that.

Won't they?

Before she could even begin to come up with answers to that troubling question, something else abruptly snagged her attention. Something on the screen of the old-timey TV. The image of snowy static that had been there since she'd entered the room abruptly disappeared, replaced by an image of a man in a black hood sitting in a shadowy room. A few seconds passed, and then he began to speak in a gravelly, artificially distorted voice.

"Good evening, and welcome to a very special Christmas at Raven's Reach . . ."

NINE

AROUND THE MANOR THAT NIGHT, in rooms strategically placed far apart, the guests paused in their various activities and discussions. Their attention was drawn to the unsettling image of the hooded man appearing on the screens of each guest's TV at the same time. The greeting from the mystery figure in no way allayed anyone's concerns regarding the still unrevealed true purpose for tonight's event at the manor. It was obvious to all that there must be more to it than awarding large cash sums to anyone who simply stayed the night. The money was only an enticement. Something else was happening here, something being kept hidden until just the right moment.

As the guests listened to the man speak in his distorted voice, many began to feel strong stirrings of anxiety and trepidation. Something wasn't right here. They all felt it in their bones, despite no explicit threat being uttered yet. They'd been tempted by the money, but now they questioned whether a more buoyant bank account was worth an unknown level of risk. For the majority of those watching, the answer to that was increasingly shifting toward an emphatic *NO*.

~

In the room he was sharing with his wife, Alan was feeling deeply troubled by multiple things even before the hooded man's speech began. He couldn't stop thinking about what he'd seen happen to the woman in the black SUV. The image of that violent moment kept flashing through his mind in an endless, vivid loop. The thing he'd seen that man do was wrong. It sickened him. He burned with a desire to *do something* about it.

Figuring out what form that action would take would have to wait, however, because he now had even bigger things weighing on his mind. After entering the manor, the Dozier family was surprised to find nobody inside waiting to greet them. Just the vast foyer, empty save for the little round table with the four stockings arranged across its surface. Each stocking had one of their names written on the cuffs in glued-on glitter. The stockings were empty, with the exception of the one bearing Alan's name. That one included a note instructing each family member to stuff the stockings with their personal cell phones and wallets. This alone earned some consternation from Sandra and the kids, but it was what followed that truly bothered Alan.

The kids were directed to stay in a separate room from their parents, which would've been fine if the rooms were adjacent to each other. They were old enough for that, and ordinarily the notion of some private adult time with Sandra would be a very appealing thing. It was something they didn't get nearly enough of at home. But the rooms *weren't* adjacent. Instead, they were in separate wings of the manor, a significant distance apart given the size and sprawl of the place. Even this *might* have been okay if they'd been allowed to keep their phones. Without that ability to instantly communicate, that distance was far more troubling.

All the mystery and weirdness about the situation was creeping Alan out in general by then. While the kids were in the midst of whining about losing access to their phones, he blurted out the suggestion that they just go home. Things were getting too strange, he told them, adding that something didn't "feel right" at Raven's Reach. Yeah, losing out on a chance at a million bucks would suck, but he'd rather be safe and sound at home with his family. They were already fifty grand richer thanks to the enticement check, which was a long way from nothing for people like them.

He was surprised by the fierceness of their opposition to the idea. All of them, Sandra and the kids. He was overreacting, they told him. Kara, his daughter, told him he was being an annoying old man. Sandra was slightly kinder, calling him a worrywart. Tommy agreed with the women of the family. In the face of their united front, there wasn't much he could do. Another kind of man, a more gruffly macho one, might've laid down the law with them, telling them they were leaving whether they liked it or not.

Alan just sighed and gave in.

And now here he was with Sandra, quietly and moodily unpacking his travel bag while his wife stood quietly over there by the huge window overlooking the dark grounds of the estate. Neither had said much to the other since entering the room about a half-hour earlier. Despite Sandra's adamantly stated desire to stay, he knew she too was troubled by the separation from their kids.

Alan stopped rooting aimlessly through his bag. "Listen, I've been thinking. I really—"

The sudden appearance of the hooded man on the screen of the old-fashioned TV distracted him, at least temporarily shutting down the effort to engage conversationally with his wife. Until then, the screen had shown only white static. He would've turned it off if not for the note taped to the top, which said leaving it on was required.

Sandra turned away from the window and approached the TV as the man began to speak.

~

"*I am your host for the evening, and my name is . . . well, that's not important right now.*" The man's distorted laugh sent a chill crawling up more than one spine as it emerged from tinny, lo-fi speakers that made it sound even more bizarre, like a recording of strange deep-space static, an unnerving signal from a distant world. "*I want to thank you all for coming tonight. As promised in the invitations most of you received . . .*" Another chuckle here, a sound that struck most watching as oddly timed or misplaced. "*. . . simply by attending tonight's exclusive event, you have earned a chance to receive a large sum of money.*" Here the hooded man leaned forward over a small desk. Before continuing, he could be seen licking his lips through the mouth-hole of the hood. "*However, contrary to what was stated in most of your invitations, you will not earn the money simply by remaining inside Raven's Reach until sunrise . . .*"

~

Unlike the other abducted "guest" staying at the manor that night, Harlan Ross did not awake to find himself chained to anything. He also had not been stripped nude. Upon stirring back to consciousness earlier that day, he found himself still in the clothes he'd been wearing Christmas Eve, but by then they were dank with his sweat. He'd spent a long stretch of hours in the grip of a dreamless, drug-induced coma. There was no clock in the room, a look out the window allowed him to surmise it was early afternoon.

After rousing himself out of the lush, canopy-covered bed, he went straight away to the door, where he found the knob unbudging. Unlike Alexandra Harcourt, he was not shy about banging on the door with the base of his fist and loudly demanding to be let out of the room. He kept at it for several minutes until he realized no one would be coming. At that point he returned to the big window and spent some time surveying the grounds of the estate.

There was no doubt he was at Raven's Reach. After first ignoring the invitations and then the threats, whoever so desperately wanted him here apparently concluded abduction was the only way. Being brought here against his will angered him immensely. He swore to himself he would make the person or persons behind it pay a harsh price.

After some more time spent fuming about it, he at last noticed the note taped to the top of the old-fashioned TV, which sat on a cart next to the wardrobe. Because he hadn't come to the manor of his own accord and therefore had not received an instructional note via stocking, this note was necessarily more verbose than the notes taped to TVs in other rooms.

A deep furrow of aggravation formed in his brow as he read the note. He was to stay in this room for the remainder of the day due to the sensitive nature of "processing" other guests who would be arriving during the afternoon and early evening. If he needed to relieve himself at any point, he was to use the chamber pot next to the bed. The author of the note expressed regret at the steps that had been necessary to ensure his presence at tonight's event and assured him he would soon understand *why* it had been necessary. He was also told not to turn off the old TV, because it would need to be on for communication purposes at some unspecified point later in the day.

Harlan crumpled the note and tossed it away in disgust.

He then spent some additional time exploring the nooks and crannies of the room in hopes of determining some other means of escape. The search was thorough, but produced nothing. The physical effort made him a bit woozy, probably because there were still traces of the knockout drug in his system. Not knowing what else to do, he decided to lie down. He immediately fell back into a deep sleep and remained there for hours, awakening mere minutes before the start of the hooded man's closed circuit in-house address to his guests.

Harlan sat up with a start as the constant field of white static on the TV screen abruptly disappeared and was replaced by the image of the hooded man in the shadowy room. He heaved himself off the bed and approached the TV as the man's distorted voice began speaking.

He listened closely, his hands clenching and unclenching as he felt his anger grow.

~

The hooded man licked his lips again, tongue sliding slowly from one side of his mouth to the other. The image playing on several screens scattered throughout the manor was not in modern high definition, but anyone viewing could nonetheless see the man's lips were dry and chapped, a condition he was finding increasingly irritating. He soon stopped speaking long enough to apply a layer of lip balm from a tube. That done, he cleared his throat and resumed speaking.

"I'm sure you are all eager to learn what tonight's exclusive event is truly all about, but I'm afraid I'm not willing to give up the game just yet. That would be spoiling all the fun, wouldn't it? In the meantime, please do try to be patient. I assure you the wait will be worth it. Or at least I believe it will." He chuckled. *"At any rate, tonight will be a special evening for all of us. Before the real fun begins, you are all cordially invited to dinner in the main dining hall. This will be a formal affair and all guests are encouraged to dress appropriately. If you did not bring formal clothes with you, suitable attire has been provided. Check the wardrobes in your rooms. Dinner is one hour from now. A timer will appear on your screens as soon as this broadcast concludes. When the timer reaches zero, your doors will unlock and you may leave your rooms at that time. Staff members will escort you to the dining hall. Until then, I bid you a good evening."*

The image of the hooded man abruptly vanished and was replaced by white numerals against a black background. The timer started at fifty minutes—50:00—and immediately started counting down from there.

~

Unlike certain others staying at Raven's Reach that night, the Martinson sisters entertained no notions of an early escape. They were as unnerved as anyone else about the strange way the evening had developed so far, but being locked in their room until dinner time was not the only thing keeping them right where they were. The door could be standing wide open and still they would feel compelled to stay in the room until given permission to leave. Like it or not, their mysterious host's knowledge and evidence of their crimes meant they were in it for the duration.

Nina had a sneer on her face as she turned away from the TV.

"What a fuckin' weirdo."

Tina looked up from buffing her nails. She was stretched out on the super-comfy bed with her head propped up on two large pillows. She smirked. "A weirdo. Right." Her tone was deadpan. "Says the girl known to occasionally insert severed body pieces inside her lady parts."

Nina let out a shivery breath of pleasure. "Oh, gosh. Why did you have to say that? Now I'm getting all tingly just thinking about it. Too bad we don't have anyone to play with."

Tina laughed.

By "play", her sister meant someone to torture and mutilate.

She shrugged. "Who knows? If it turns out this guy in the hood is a fan of our work, maybe he'll let us have some fun with these other guests that are supposedly here."

The note of skepticism in her voice was only there because they still had yet to see anyone else at the manor. No guests. No staff. No one at all. Nor had they heard any voices or sounds of movement from the long hallway outside their room. It was downright eerie, even for a woman who'd spent most of her life as a predator.

Nina wandered over to the big window and stared down at the dark grounds at the rear of the property. "I wonder if there are any bodies buried down there in that garden. That's where I'd bury the jerks if we lived here."

"Jerks" was a word they often used in place of "victim" or any of that word's common synonyms, because in their view they were jerks for being dumb enough to let themselves get killed. Jerks for letting themselves get so easily lured into obviously dangerous situations. It was part of their shared terminology of killing, which was extensive after being at it for twenty years.

Tina chortled. "Nah. Too obvious. Haven't you ever seen a mystery movie? That'd be the first place the cops checked if they ever came out to dig up the property."

Nina turned away from the window. "So what would you do with them?"

"The jerks?"

"Yeah."

Tina shrugged and resumed buffing her nails. "I guess if I had the money to buy a giant-ass mansion like this, I'd have a crematorium installed somewhere on the property, maybe in some secret room under the house. Then I'd just burn the jerks down to nothing and scatter their ashes in the woods."

Nina grunted. "Huh. That actually sounds kind of fucking awesome. If we really walk out of here with a million bucks, we've gotta get a place in the country somewhere. A *big* place. Oh, shit! I know!" She snapped her fingers and her voice rose sharply in pitch. "We'll quit our jobs and start a funeral home! It'd be the perfect fucking cover!"

Tina stared at her sister in a stupefied way that soon transitioned to smiling awe. "Holy shit. That's actually a great idea."

Nina did a goofy little happy dance. "I know!"

As the sisters began to excitedly discuss all the thrilling possibilities of Nina's sudden brainstorm, the counter on the TV screen reached the 40:00 mark.

~

Alexandra Harcourt stared numbly at the TV as the numerals on the screen ticked down to 39:00 and kept on going. She was sitting on the floor with her knees pulled up to her chest and her back against the foot of the bed. It was the same position she'd been in for going on thirty minutes.

She felt out of it, on the brink of total mental collapse and barely able to process the full meaning behind the words uttered by the man who'd appeared on the TV a short while ago. His message seemed to suggest several other people were currently "guests" at the manor. In her mind, that word was in quotes, because she believed it was used in place of words with more sinister meanings. A word, for instance, like abductee. Were these other so-called guests here of their own free will or had they, like her, been snatched from their homes and brought to this place without their consent?

Before she could give much thought to that, a key rattled in the lock and the door to her room began to creakily swing open. Bright light slanting in from the hallway made her squint as a dark shape stepped into the room. This man was shorter than the lanky person who'd pushed the cart into the room earlier. He was also noticeably less slender than that man. Like that man, however, he wore a black hood over his head. He also wore a long black cloak that reached to his ankles. The hardwood floor creaked beneath his tread as he moved across the room to stand in front of her.

Alexandra trembled as she stared up at the man, who stood about six feet away. His eyes and mouth were visible through slits cut in the black cloth. There was something very intense about his eyes. They roamed all over her body in a way that made her glad she'd pulled her knees up to her chest, thereby covering her breasts. The man's breathing steadily became more audible. He licked his lips repeatedly and appeared to tremble. She wondered if something was wrong with him until she saw the movement at the front of his cloak. When she realized he had a hand loose inside the cloak and was beating off, she made a loud sound of disgust and called him a fucking pervert. As soon as she said those words, he moaned and then gasped, hunching over slightly in a way that made it perfectly clear what had just happened.

Alexandra recoiled, pulling her knees even tighter to her chest. "You sick fucking bastard! What the fuck is wrong with you?"

The man licked his lips and stared at her in leering silence for a moment. Then he giggled like a little schoolboy being naughty on the playground at recess and scurried out of the room like a bug, slamming and locking the door behind him.

TEN

BRADLEY WINTHORPE LET OUT A breath as the TV counter ticked down to 0:00 and stayed there. An instant later, he heard a click from the door and knew it was now unlocked. Rather than going to it immediately, he turned away from the TV and checked himself in the full-length floor mirror one last time.

His hair was immaculate and the Armani suit from the wardrobe looked perfectly tailored to fit his trim build. Any thought of wearing the suit he'd brought with him was abandoned as soon as he opened the wardrobe and got a look at the beautiful clothes hanging inside. If anything, the Armani suit looked slightly better than his own suit, which actually *had* been tailored to fit him. Strange, perhaps, but not something worth questioning at this point.

He wished he still had the Walther PPK he'd been instructed to surrender as a condition of staying at the manor. That sense of something off he'd felt upon arriving at the place had only intensified during the hours of waiting, leaving him convinced there must be some nefarious intent behind the event supposedly happening tonight. A *lot* was wrong here at Raven's Reach, but he was in the thick of it now, and the only thing he could do was see this strange adventure through to the end. Still, the weight of that gun strapped to his body would have made him feel better.

After running a hand down the front of his suit jacket one more time, he went to the door and opened it. A man in a black hood stood opposite the door on the other side of the wide hallway. He stared evenly at Bradley but said nothing. The rest of the man's attire was the formal wear of a butler or valet, down to his polished shoes and the white gloves on his hands. He certainly looked the part of a person one would imagine working at a place like Raven's Reach. Other than the hood, that is. That was just creepy.

Bradley cleared his throat. "I assume you're to be my escort to the dining hall."

The man nodded. "This way."

He turned away from Bradley and started walking down the hallway at a leisurely pace. Bradley followed at the same unhurried pace, choosing to stay slightly behind the man rather than walk alongside him.

"Say, um . . . are you the guy who did the weird greeting speech via vintage television a little bit ago? Because I'm thinking you're not."

The man remained facing forward as he said, "I am not."

Bradley nodded. "Yeah. Like I said, didn't think so." He paused a beat. "Had to ask, though, because of the, you know . . . the hood."

The man grunted but said nothing.

They walked along in silence for the next several strides, until Bradley cleared his throat again and said, "So . . . these hoods, what's the deal? Why wear them? I mean, identity concealment, right? I get that. But why is that necessary? What are you people hiding?"

Even as he was speaking, Bradley regretted the words coming out of his mouth. He'd planned to play it cool and keep mostly quiet until he had a better idea what was going on, but his jumpy nerves were getting the better of him. He kept thinking about his debt to the mob guys and again wondered if they might be behind all this. For all he knew, the guy walking ahead of him might be leading him to his execution. The idea sent a shiver of fear rippling through him, but he was still mostly convinced there was something else behind all this. If the mob wanted him dead, they wouldn't go to this much trouble. Wouldn't be worth the time or expense. He'd just get popped outside his place of work one day or blown up by a car bomb. Still, unlikely though it seemed, the possibility was just one more thing making him anxious.

The man again didn't glance back at him as he said, "I'm sorry, sir. It's not my place to say."

Bradley nodded. "Right, right. Of course not. Forget I asked."

He kept quiet the rest of the way to the dining hall, which was on the ground floor of the manor. After descending one of the twin spiral staircases down to the foyer, they continued down the hallway between the staircases. Unlike upstairs, the floor here was black and white tiles in a checkerboard pattern. The walls were painted a deep shade of red, and the passage was lit by lamps in ornate wall sconces. They passed multiple closed doors en route to the dining hall and he idly wondered what might be behind them.

Up ahead on the left, he spied a wide entryway through which bright light was visible. Given that the room beyond the entryway was at the end of the hallway, he made an educated guess that this was the dining hall. Within another few seconds, he began to perceive a low rumble of voices. Some of the other guests must already be inside. He was curious to learn whether any of them would be people he knew. Business associates, perhaps. There must be *something* connecting all the invitees to the event, even if it was a tenuous thing.

Out of nowhere, a possibility that hadn't previously occurred to him popped into his head. Back in their younger days, growing up and all the way through college, his older brother, Tod, was quite the prankster. He was always working people up and pulling off-the-wall shit. After graduating Princeton, over twenty years ago now, all that had come to an end, seemingly forever, but what if the prankster had decided to come out of retirement with a big splash? What if this was some elaborate surprise family reunion thing? It'd been a while since they'd all reassembled for Christmas, after all. Four long years had passed since the last time the Winthorpes had gathered to celebrate the season.

Sure, it fit.

Almost too perfectly, in fact.

Bradley briefly stopped in his tracks before reaching the entryway, suddenly sure he'd hit on something close to the truth. For the first time, his escort stopped walking and glanced back at him. "Something wrong?"

Bradley swallowed hard and spoke in a quieter tone than he'd been using, hoping he wouldn't be heard by anyone in the dining hall. "I'm not sure I want to do this after all. I suddenly have the sinking feeling there are people I don't want to see in there."

The man stared blankly at him a moment before sighing. "It's a little too late for second thoughts, sir. You also don't actually have a choice. Please. I'd rather not have to drag you in there."

Bradley frowned. "You'd really do that?"

"Yes, sir."

Bradley sighed. "I suppose I should spare us both that embarrassment."

The man nodded. "Yes, sir."

Because he'd surrendered both the gun and his keys upon entering the manor, Bradley was left with no obvious viable alternative to doing as the man said. Sure, he could turn tail and run, but what good would that do? Even if he could get out of the house—something he definitely wasn't sure about—he would be faced with the daunting prospect of getting back to town on foot. He would first have to get off the property and then down the long and treacherous access road. If he could manage that, he would then have to walk nearly twenty more miles until reaching Thornton. Besides that, it was Christmas day in a rural area. People were inside with their families. The odds of successfully hitching a ride were slim to none. If he somehow did make it to Thornton despite all these hindrances, he would be without his wallet and phone.

Fuck.

Bradley shrugged. "All right. Fuck it. Let's do this."

They resumed walking and in another few moments rounded the corner into the dining hall, where several people were already gathered. One woman who was standing with her back turned toward him turned around and gasped when she saw him.

Then she screamed.

ELEVEN

WHEN THE BLACK-HOOODED MAN on the screen finished speaking and the countdown clock appeared in his place, Colette was overcome with a lightheaded feeling so pronounced she briefly felt like she was coming untethered from the world. From existence itself. She was close to flopping over into the still slowly spreading pool of blood on the floor when something primal inside her asserted control and brought her swiftly back from the brink. It was like being shocked out of a trance with a massive dose of adrenaline.

She felt jittery and not just from the recent violent struggle with George.

Her life of comfortable privilege had taken a sudden and unexpected dizzying turn into surrealist nightmare territory. She was trapped with a corpse in a locked room in a sprawling gothic manor. She'd just watched a man in a black hood deliver a strange speech in a voice that made him sound like a demonic robot. The TV that had delivered the speech to her room looked like a relic from the 70s and was perhaps even older. She didn't have her phone and she was hundreds of miles removed from anyone who could feasibly help her, more vulnerable than she could remember ever being during her adult life. All these things made sense only as random ingredients in a bad dream, one she would surely wake up from at any moment.

She waited.

Watched the countdown clock as several minutes rolled away. Nothing changed.

She pinched her arm and yelped.

"Fuck!"

The time to pull herself together and confront the truth had arrived. This was no bad dream. It was reality and she needed to start thinking hard about her next moves. The last thing she wanted was to wind up in jail for murder. Even if she wasn't convicted for it—and she thought her odds were good on that count, being a person of immense wealth—the scandal of it all would follow her the rest of her life. No more getting invited to all the best parties and high-profile social functions. She might even be forced to give up her board of directors' seat at David's former company. The buyout would be lucrative, but she would be surrendering a position of power the likes of which she would never hold again. Most galling of all was the thought of losing all of that for killing someone like George Barrington, a vacuous and useless waste of space.

More minutes rolled off the countdown clock.

She was running out of time to prepare herself for the dinner.

Her eyes darted around the room a few moments in a frantic search for answers that weren't coming immediately to mind. She would need to get rid of the body entirely before she left this place. Perhaps have it dismembered and burned and then buried out in the woods. She knew immediately this was something she wouldn't be able to do on her own. She would have to recruit help from someone else staying at the manor tonight. Another guest or a member of the staff. Approaching someone else would come with great risk. That person might later blackmail her or go to the police. Her increasing anxiety about the shrinking amount of time she had caused her to shake off this concern. She would have to circle back to the issue of corpse disposal later.

Right at this moment, however, what mattered most was getting the body out of sight and the mess cleaned up. The space under the bed looked large enough to accommodate George. It was her only viable option because she couldn't see herself lifting her dead lover up and stashing him in the wardrobe. She was a slender woman who weighed in at around 110 pounds. George's body was two hundred and some pounds of dead weight. It was an equation that wouldn't work no matter how you looked at it.

After getting to her feet long enough to remove her dress and kick off her shoes, she dropped to her knees again and got to work pushing the body across the floor toward the bed. Sweat rose on her brow and pooled in her armpits. She grimaced, knowing her makeup would be ruined before the job was done. It was just one more thing to address before it was time to leave the room. The physical exertion necessary to get the body under the bed caused her to grunt repeatedly. To her ears, she sounded like a female tennis pro bouncing around a court at Wimbledon, a mental association that brought back memories of her late husband. David often had watched tennis on TV and she'd never been able to fathom why. It was so boring. Only televised golf was more tedious, in her view. This was a symptom of an ongoing theme in her life. The men she took as lovers always seemed to have such painfully dull interests and hobbies. It was a wonder she didn't wind up killing more of them.

Once she had the body stashed as far under the bed as she could manage, she turned her attention to the pool of blood. Parts of the body had passed through it while being moved, resulting in crimson smears across a wide swath of the hardwood floor. She would need a mop and bucket to clean up that much of it, maybe some towels, too. Unfortunately, she had none of those things available. Another frantic scan of the room led to just one possible solution, and a temporary one at that.

A large throw rug took up much of the floor space between the foot of the bed and the wardrobe. She yanked it up and dragged it over to the side of the bed, draping it over the smeared pool of blood. The rug obscured most of it, but some was still visible between the edge of the rug and the bed. She opened George's travel bag and rooted through his clothes, pulling out a salmon-colored Polo shirt.

Good enough.

She dropped to her knees again and went to work scrubbing up as much of the visible blood as she could. A few minutes of work resulted in a more than adequate job. Any casual glance into the room would reveal nothing amiss. She stuffed the bloody shirt in George's bag, zipped the bag up, and tossed it under the bed.

She hurried over to the wardrobe and selected one of the fine dresses provided by her host. A stunning backless red one she figured was appropriate in a macabre way, given what she'd been doing over the last several minutes. She set the dress aside and hurriedly went to work fixing her face. By the time she was finished, less than five minutes remained on the countdown clock. She donned the dress and a reserve set of heels more appropriate to the color of her selected attire.

The countdown clock reached zero.

The door unlocked with an audible click.

She went out to the hallway where her escort was waiting and preemptively addressed the absence of her companion. "My partner won't be joining us tonight. He's taken rather severely ill."

To her great relief, the woman in the red hood did not challenge this assertion. "That's quite all right. You're the important one, after all."

Colette's spirits were buoyed slightly by hearing this.

That's right, she thought. *I am* the important one. *George is irrelevant. Nobody cares about him. Not even his father. Everything's going to be fine. Just fine.*

She followed the woman in red down to the dining hall.

TWELVE

TO SAY THE DINING hall was a much larger space than Alan Dozier imagined would be vastly understating things. The entire main dining area of a nice restaurant would fit in here. Rather than the one long table he'd anticipated, multiple smaller tables were arranged in a loose circle in the approximate center of the space, with wide gaps between each table. He wondered if this might be a way of deflecting attention from what might otherwise have been a distractingly large amount of empty space. Probably so, he supposed, but it was only a minimally successful attempt at best.

Sandra clutched at his arm and put her mouth close to his ear. "Jesus Christ, babe. This place is *huge*. You could fit an army in here."

Alan nodded: "I was thinking practically the same damn thing. All this for so few people? It's downright weird."

It appeared he and Sandra were the first invitees to arrive in the dining hall. A pristine white tablecloth was draped over each table. The amount of fabric hanging over the sides was more than generous. A person could hide under any of these tables without being detected, at least until everyone else arrived and took their seats. A wild impulse to hurriedly check under them all came and went. He would hate to be caught in the act of doing such a goofy thing for no good reason.

The decision to exercise restraint in this matter was shown to be a wise one just seconds later, when their escort returned to the dining hall after disappearing for a few minutes. Except, no, that wasn't exactly true. Alan did a double-take as he abruptly realized this wasn't actually the same person as before. The attire was the same and this person's build was similar, but he was at least a few inches shorter. The source of his confusion was those damn hoods. It bothered him that these people were hiding their faces. What was the point? People who robbed banks or burglarized homes did that. People who were criminals.

Were these people criminals?

Alan frowned hard, mulling the question over as this second hooded person guided them to what he called their "assigned" table, which had two chairs and two place settings. He snapped out of it when Sandra voiced her disapproval.

"Oh, this won't do. Our children will be joining us. We'll need a different table. A bigger one. Or we'll have to push two of these together."

The man's gaze stayed on them for an uncomfortably long silent stretch before he said, "Push two of them together? This isn't Cracker Barrel, lady. This is your assigned table. You will sit where you're told to sit." His cold smile was visible through the mouth-hole of his hood. "Noncompliance will result in forfeiture of your chance at the prize."

Sandra's eyes narrowed to slits as her pretty face twisted in a scowl. "I don't think I like your tone, mister. I'm a guest here. Show respect."

Alan smiled in a strained way as he took the rare step of interjecting when his wife was angry at someone. "We don't like the arrangement one bit, but we can put up with it for as long as it takes to sit down and eat. Isn't that right, dear?"

He felt the rage radiating from Sandra as she turned toward him, but he gave her a look that amounted to a non-verbal equivalent of begging. She'd seen the look enough times to know what it meant. Her own features shifted in a way he knew indicated reluctant acquiescence. She was still ultra-pissed, but she would set that aside temporarily for his sake.

She sighed. "Fine. We'll sit here."

"In the meantime," Alan said, striving for a sterner tone of reprimand as he addressed the hooded servant again. "Don't let me hear you disrespect my wife that way again. I won't stand for it. Got that?"

The sharp curve of the man's lips made it clear he was trying hard not to laugh in Alan's face. Instead, he bowed slightly and took his leave of them. There was a hint of insolent sarcasm in that bow. Alan saw it, and if he saw it, no way in hell had Sandra missed it.

She made a sound of disgust, shaking her head. "That fucking asshole."

Alan nodded.

His heart was still racing. That verbal rebuke of the servant was something he'd only ever dared to attempt a few times in his life. Doing it now made his stomach feel funny. He was a little lightheaded, too. But he also felt proud of himself. Maybe this interaction would help him find the nerve to stand up to that other guest's abusive companion should the need arise.

They'd just sat at their table when Alan was distracted by voices emanating from the hallway. Female voices, from the sound of it. Turning his head in that direction, he saw yet another hooded man in formal servant attire enter the dining hall ahead of two stunningly gorgeous women. One woman was blonde and the other had hair dyed a shade of midnight black. They wore clingy dresses with short hems, a stark contrast to the more modest dress worn by his wife. The blonde's dress was blue, while her companion wore, perhaps predictably, black. Otherwise, however, the women looked like exact clones of each other.

Twins, Alan thought. *They're hot twin sisters. Jesus Christ.*

The ladies saw him staring and came over to introduce themselves, high heels clacking on the hardwood floor.

The blonde arrived first, smiling as she extended a hand to Alan. "Hi, I'm Tina."

Alan realized his mouth was hanging open. Suddenly afraid of coming across like an unsophisticated rube, he closed it and swallowed a lump in his throat. Then he took the proffered hand and held it limply as he said, "Um, I'm, uh . . ." *Oh, shit,* he thought, *what's my name?* He experienced some moments of intensely disorienting confusion on the subject before the answer appeared in his head like glowing letters typed on a screen. "Alan. Alan . . . Dozier. And this . . ." He indicated Sandra with a tilt of his head. ". . . is Sandra. My wife."

The wattage of the blonde's smile hadn't slipped at all while Alan fumbled. "Well, hello, Al and Sandy. It's so awesome to meet both of you."

Her thumb slowly rubbed the back of Alan's hand in a way that was difficult to take as anything other than overtly flirtatious. The black-haired sister came over and shook his hand in a similar way.

"And I'm Nina. Isn't this such a cool place?"

Her thumb rubbed the back of his hand while her fingers tickled the underside of his wrist, raising goosebumps on his arm. In his more than twenty years with Sandra, he'd never once cheated on her. In that moment, however, he knew he would succumb to either of these women given the chance. He felt bad for even allowing the thought to enter his head, but feeling bad didn't change the truth of it.

Nina squeezed his hand before relinquishing her grip on it. "Good to meet you, Al. Let's hang out later."

Alan had no idea how to respond to that—not with an undoubtedly stewing mad Sandra sitting right next to him—so he didn't say anything. He reluctantly turned toward his wife as the sisters allowed their escort to lead them to their assigned table. He dreaded the anticipated look of fury on her face, but to his surprise, she was only smirking in an amused, almost playful way.

He frowned. "What, you're not pissed at me for drooling over them?"

Sandra leaned close and dropped her voice to a whisper. "I hate to break it to you, babe, but you weren't the only one drooling over them." She slipped a hand under the table, gripping his knee. Her lips got closer to his ear, almost brushing against it. "Tell you what. If you can convince either of them to come to bed with us, I'm all for it."

Alan shivered.

He couldn't believe what he was hearing. Not once in all their years together had she suggested anything like this, nor had she ever conveyed even the tiniest hint of sexual attraction to anyone who wasn't a man. It was confusing and exciting at the same time. If she'd suddenly sprouted a pair of wings and started flying around the room, he would've been less surprised. "Are you serious?"

She chuckled softly and squeezed his knee again. "Think of it as a one-time escape from reality. We've got that room all to ourselves. The kids will never know."

Alan couldn't help grinning.

He was still thinking it all over when the scream rang out, a shrill noise that made him jump in his chair. Glancing around, he saw that someone else had come into the dining hall. This time it was a man unaccompanied by anyone other than yet another hooded escort. The guy had a slick look about him and a palpably snobbish way of carrying himself. Alan figured he was a bigshot investor or banking executive, something like that. Not that he actually knew much about that world. The man just looked the way those people often looked when portrayed in movies.

One of the sisters babbled excitedly as she went racing over to him. It was Tina, the blonde. Apparently she knew the guy, because she threw her arms around him and said something about how good it was to see him again after all this time. The guy smiled as he briefly embraced her, but Alan detected a clear level of strain in the expression. He was shocked by the presence of this old acquaintance and was trying to fake being happy about it. The charade continued as Nina came over and also exchanged greetings with the banker-looking guy.

Before long, one of the hooded servants intervened, gently encouraging the three of them to take their seats at their respective tables, which they soon did after a few additional moments of banal chit-chat. The banker-looking guy didn't bother introducing himself to the Doziers as the servant guided him to a table with a lone place setting. Alan found it hard to take that as anything other than a deliberate snub, which, as far as he was concerned, validated the instinctive dislike he felt for the man.

Their kids were the next guests to enter the dining hall and Alan felt an immense relief sweep over him the instant he saw them. His eyes got a little wetter than usual as they hurried over. He and Sandra came out of their chairs and took turns embracing their children. Sandra asked about a million rapid-fire questions before anyone else could speak. Tommy did most of the responding, confirming that their room was fine and that nothing worrisome had happened while they were apart. Kara was quieter and discernibly less enthused about everything than her brother, but that was normal for her.

Their escort—hooded, like all the rest—allowed this to continue for slightly more than a full minute before loudly clearing his throat and announcing that it was time for the younger Doziers to proceed to their own table. Sandra glared at the man briefly but didn't get testy with him. The Doziers exchanged goodbyes and within another few seconds the kids were on their way.

When Alan was sitting again, he glanced around and noticed that Tina was staring right at him. Her expression was oddly blank, but she smiled when they made eye contact. "Cute kids."

Alan nodded. "Thanks."

"Yeah, totally," the other one, Nina, added. "And, hey, forgive me if I'm out of line here, but neither of them really takes after you at all. Like, not even a little bit. You sure the missus wasn't having it on with the mailman or the cable guy when she got knocked up with these two?"

Al's smile faded. "What?"

Sandra pushed her chair back from the table and turned it toward the sisters. "That's the rudest goddamn thing anyone has ever said to me."

If anything, hearing Sandra talk this way within earshot of the kids was even more shocking to Al than Nina's rudeness. He couldn't remember her ever doing that. Maybe a "damn" or a "hell" once in a blue moon, but never the big G-D. This development was *bad* with a capital B.

Nina chuckled. "I didn't say it to you, honey."

The sisters glanced at each other and giggled like schoolgirls.

A breath hissed between Sandra's tightly clenched teeth as she began to rise from her chair. Alan put a hand on her shoulder and kept her from rising any further. "Ignore them. They're not worth it."

Tina laughed. "Oh, come on, you don't mean that. We were getting along so well a minute ago." She locked eyes with him and winked. "My sister was just joking. Playing around. She likes being inappropriate just to get a rise out of people. It's like a hobby of hers."

Nina nodded. "Yeah, Sandy, I was just playing. I mean, I said 'forgive me' right at the beginning, remember? You really need to lighten up."

Alan's hand was still on his wife's shoulder. He could feel her muscles tensing up again. She felt like a snake getting ready to strike. His heart was racing at just the prospect of a fight breaking out. His mind raced too as he struggled and failed to think of a way to defuse things.

Sandra unclenched her teeth and spoke in a tightly controlled tone. "I guess I don't understand why you think it's okay to be so rude and thoughtless to a complete stranger, even if you were just *playing*."

Heavy sarcasm on that last word.

Alan's priority here, of course, remained coming up with a way to defuse a potentially volatile and embarrassing situation. In the back of his mind, however, was a severe pang of regret at knowing his chance of a threesome with his wife and one of the astoundingly hot sisters was dead. His disappointment was tempered, however, by the subsequent realization that it'd probably never been a real possibility at all. In fact, he had a feeling the sisters had been playing with them from the moment they walked into the room.

Nina smirked. "Honestly, I really was only joking around, but I seem to have hit a nerve." Her gaze shifted to Alan. "Interesting. Very interesting."

Alan glanced over at his kids, who were watching the exchange with nearly identical expressions of mortification. He tried to think of some reassuring words for them, but before any could come to mind, another person was escorted into the dining hall.

The new arrival was another man attending without a companion. Any resemblance to the banker-type person ended right there. This man was taller and burlier, at least a few inches over six feet. He wasn't exactly fat, but he had a slightly protruding belly that suggested a healthy appetite. He had a lot of bushy black hair and a thick beard and mustache to match. A tie was loosely knotted around his neck, but he'd opted not to wear a blazer. The sloppiness of his attire along with his general appearance made him come across like a crotchety high school civics teacher. His thick-framed glasses only enhanced this impression.

All eyes were on this man as he followed an escort to a table on the opposite side of the loose circle. Rather than immediately sitting down, the man took a halfhearted stab at straightening his tie as he cleared his throat and addressed the room in a deep baritone. "My name is Harlan Ross, and I don't know about the rest of you motherfucking assholes, but I would like to make it known that I am here under duress. And by that I mean I was abducted and drugged in the middle of the night, all because I ignored and declined the invitations the rest of you swine undoubtedly accepted due to being greedy pieces of shit."

And with that, he pulled out a chair and sat down.

THIRTEEN

THE NEXT GUEST TO ENTER the dining hall was Colette Hammerschmidt. She summoned a small, aloof smile as she followed her escort and nodded once in a curt way at the other attendees. She maintained the expression as her gaze swept over their faces and realized a few were faintly familiar. These included the big man with the scruffy look, the sisters in the scandalously small dresses, and another man who looked a bit like a refugee from the stock market trenches of Wall Street. The others, a pair of teenagers and an average-looking couple who were maybe their parents, were not familiar to her in the least.

She was still trying to work out how she knew the familiar-looking ones when her escort—apparently the only female on staff at Raven's Reach and definitely the only one wearing a full-body red catsuit—stopped at a table with two place settings and pulled out a chair for her. Sitting here would put her between the sexy sisters and the man who looked like a banker or stock broker. She took her seat at the table and again scanned the faces arrayed around her as her escort swiftly departed the dining hall.

There was a palpable tension in the room she initially ascribed to the unusual setting and circumstances. That was undoubtedly a factor, but it didn't take long to deduce something else was at work here. Some of these people were furious at each other. She read it in their body language and in the looks some of them were exchanging. The woman who looked like a standard middle-class housewife looked ready to explode. She was absolutely seething with rage. Judging from the direction of her gaze, it appeared the twin sisters were the object of her ire. For their part, the smirking sisters appeared utterly unfazed. Amused, even.

Colette cleared her throat. "Oh, dear. I seem to have walked into an awkward situation."

The sisters giggled in an affected schoolgirl manner. It was a sound Colette knew well, being one she frequently heard from certain women in her social circle back home. Women in early middle-age trying too hard to sound younger than they actually were. These two were undeniably gorgeous, but even for them, advancing age was starting to show in small ways. They were probably conscious of that and therefore overcompensating. She knew she looked outwardly older than they did, but she suspected they were in the same general age bracket. That was when it hit her, her eyes widening as the names surged up from one of the hidden, buried places in her mind.

Tina and Nina Martinson.

The notorious mean girl twins of Stockdale High School, class of 1999.

Oh, shit.

At that point, the floodgates of memory opened wide. Her eyes flicked around the room again. The scruffy-looking big guy was Harlan Ross, class clown and editor-in-chief of the school paper. The banker or whatever was Bradley Winthorpe, senior year homecoming king runner-up. In 1997, she'd given Bradley a handjob in the back of an orange Firebird. Thinking about it put her back in that moment in a disconcertingly vivid way. She could almost taste the orange Mad Dog 20/20 he'd been drinking that night as she remembered how his tongue felt sliding into her mouth. The make-out session went on long enough to leave a lasting impression mostly because he took forever to come. When it finally happened, his release spurted high enough to stain the front of her new blouse. That was the end of their one-week fling, but that wasn't the only way they were indelibly connected. The other thing was a connection they both shared with Harlan and the Martinson sisters. They were all part of the same crowd, an exclusive clique of popular kids who all thought they were better than everybody else.

Kids who could get away with just about anything.

The "Kool Klub", as they'd called themselves. God, how cringe-worthy that name seemed now. How had they ever taken it seriously?

Colette shuddered at the thought of it. More old memories tried to crowd into the forefront of her mind, including one she suspected at least partly explained the real reason she and her old classmates had been summoned to this place. It wasn't about money at all. That was only a ruse. This was all about a long-delayed reckoning with the past, one she'd allowed herself to believe would never happen. Not after so many years. The presence of Mr. and Mrs. Suburban Goober and their kids confused her slightly. They obviously had no connection to the sins of Stockdale High's in-crowd circa 1999. Of course, it was possible whoever had invited Colette to Raven's Reach had some other, unrelated grievance against the seemingly out-of-place couple. It was the only thing that made sense, really.

She glanced over at the entryway to the dining hall. Multiple black-hooded servants were standing around over there, closely watching the guests in a way that suggested they were ready to intervene should anyone attempt to leave without permission. Another hooded servant stood over by the door at the back of the room, one she assumed led to the kitchen. Until now, those hoods seemed only vaguely sinister, just another part of the employees' official garb. Strange, but not overly worrisome. Now, however, she understood just how wrong she'd been about that. Not just wrong, but dangerously naive.

The people in hoods weren't anything as innocuous as normal servants. They were guards and enforcers. Thugs hiding behind a ve-neer of upper-class servility. All of whom were undoubtedly comfort-able with engaging in acts of violence should the need arise. And with George out of the picture, she had no one she could rely on for pro-tection. The coward probably wouldn't have been much good in that department anyway, but he would've been better than nothing. Maybe.

The awkward tension in the room had not abated. The housewife was still smoldering. The sisters were still smirking. Bradley remained as silent as the rest, but he was looking at her in a curious way now. In another moment or two, he'd probably make the connection.

Before that could happen, the housewife's husband broke the si-lence. "Hold on just a damn minute. You're saying you were kid-napped and brought here? Is that a joke?"

Colette followed the man's gaze and realized he was addressing Harlan Ross.

Harlan grunted. "I am indeed saying that, sir. I would not joke about such a thing."

A deep furrow formed in the middle of the other man's brow as his confusion deepened. "But I don't understand. Why would someone do that?"

Harlan took a slow look around the room before replying. His gaze lingered on Colette a noticeable beat longer than the rest. "That's an excellent question," he said, when his gaze again settled on the husband. "Given that many of us here tonight knew each other long ago, I have my suspicions."

The husband leaned forward, his slight pudge pushing against the edge of his table. "Yeah, I caught on already that some of you weren't exactly total strangers. What could these suspicions of yours possibly have to do with me and my family?"

Harlan shrugged. "About that, I haven't a clue. As for my suspicions, I don't care to share them at this time, a sentiment I'm sure I share with each of my former classmates gathered here tonight."

Having tuned into the conversation Harlan was having with her husband, the housewife broke off her staring contest with the sisters and focused on the bespectacled big man. "Oh, fuck that. It feels like we got lured out here on false fucking pretenses. We've got goons hiding their faces and looming over us like damn vultures. I'm starting to think my kids might be in real danger, and you've got the goddamn gall to tell me you know something and refuse to say what it is? Well, I say again, fuck that. You spill the beans right now or I'm coming over there to wring your damn neck."

The sisters giggled in their usual schoolgirl way at the conclusion of this speech.

Colette had a small chuckle of her own. Still smiling, she glanced over at Harlan. "Oh, my. You are in real trouble now, Harley."

He looked at her, his expression solemn but not entirely devoid of warmth. "No one has called me that in a very long time. I'm not happy about being here for many reasons, but it is not an entirely unpleasant thing seeing you again."

The housewife thumped her fist down on her table, making silverware rattle. "No! You do *not* get to ignore me, asshole!" She picked up a steak knife and waved it at him. "Spill your guts before I spill them for you."

Nina laughed in a more adult way this time. "Someone's got anger management issues. Don't mind her. She's still upset about getting called out for being a cheating whore."

Colette found herself wishing for some wine to sip while watching this amusing drama unfold. There was a glass on the table, but it was empty. Too bad. Despite her own multi-layered concerns over the situation at Raven's Reach, she was feeling entertained. It seemed the Martinson sisters retained their old penchant for cruelly getting under the skin of people they felt were beneath them. People who were inferior. She still had a clear memory of Nina waving a hundred-dollar bill in a bum's face and then having her boyfriend of the time beat the man bloody when he tried to snatch it from her fingers. Back then, Colette always got a big kick out of watching them do their thing. In that way at least, nothing had changed.

The housewife glared at Nina, her fingers turning red as they clenched tighter around the handle of the knife. "Oh, I haven't forgotten about you, little missy. No one insults my family like that and gets away with it. I'll deal with you soon enough."

Nina did a mock shiver and laughed. "Ooohh, I'm so scared."

"You fucking well should be." The housewife's gaze returned to Harlan. "You've got about ten seconds to start talking."

Harlan gave her a perplexed look. "Madam, are you threatening me with physical violence?"

The woman sneered. "I absolutely am."

Bradley interjected for the first time. "Everyone please just calm down."

Everyone ignored this as Harlan stared evenly back at the woman for a period of several silent seconds. His expression was thoughtful, but he did not seem overly distressed regarding the potential of any actual harm to his person.

He shrugged. "In light of the highly unusual nature of this gathering, I suppose I see no harm in putting all my cards on the table. I'm sure the authorities will never—"

And that was when the lights went out.

FOURTEEN

THERE WERE STARTLED GASPS AND cries of surprise as blackness enveloped the room. This was followed by an excited babble of voices as many in the room wondered aloud what was happening. Bradley did not add his own voice to the chorus of distress. The power had gone out. So what? There was nothing sinister about that and he saw no reason to get worked up about it. Raven's Reach was way up in the mountains. Outages probably happened on a semi-regular basis. Someone on staff would undoubtedly get a generator going and the lights would be back on soon enough.

Meanwhile, he would take advantage of the momentary distraction by trying to talk some sense into Harlan Ross. The man seemed on the brink of talking about things they'd all agreed to never talk about again. Not to strangers and not even among themselves. Things best left buried for the rest of their lives. It was a vow Bradley had never broken. He rarely even allowed himself to think about that long ago night. He'd almost managed to forget any of it had ever happened. Bringing it all out into the open, even in this limited way, would be a terrible mistake.

He got up from his chair and took a few careful steps in Harlan's direction. "Hey, Harlan," he said, keeping his voice low but hopefully at a level his old friend could hear through the surrounding din of conversation. "Can I talk to you a minute?"

He heard the big man sigh heavily.

Before Harlan could say anything, however, shouts erupted from the other side of the room. The shouts were followed by sounds of struggle. Silverware rattled as someone bumped hard against a table. A man was yelling at someone to get off of him. That could be no one other than the irate housewife's husband. The housewife was yelling, too, with an ear-splitting shrillness that set Bradley's teeth on edge. The husband's shouts cut off abruptly, followed by a choking sound and a wet gurgle. Then came a heavy thump. In the midst of all this was a sound of feet running away. This was followed by the slamming of a door and after that a sound of something ratcheting downward on rollers. When the lights popped back on an instant later, Bradley was staring right at the way out to the hallway, only now it was blocked off.

Someone had pulled down a roll door.

And now people were screaming again, seemingly louder than ever. Bradley heard Harlan sigh again and say, "Oh, dear lord."

Bradley turned and followed his gaze. "Oh, shit."

The housewife's husband was slumped over the table, blood gurgling through the hands clamped around his throat. As Bradley watched, the man twitched a final time or two and went still. One of his hands came away from his throat, revealing the wide slit of a knife.

FIFTEEN

HARLAN GRIMACED AS HE OBSERVED the anguish of the woman who'd been berating him with such ferocity just a few moments ago. Her face was flushed red and her eyes were filled with tears as she wailed in denial of the grisly reality of her husband's death. That he was indeed dead and beyond hope of resuscitation was obvious to anyone without an emotional connection to the man. Even a team of skilled EMTs with all the tools at their disposal would be unable to do anything about the gaping hole in his neck, but that didn't stop the new widow from trying anyway.

She grabbed napkins from the table and desperately pressed them to the man's neck in a last-ditch effort to stem the draining away of his life's blood. By then, however, the torrent of bright crimson had slowed to a trickle, which Harlan knew meant the man's heart was no longer beating. The teenagers hovered around the table as their mother continued her doomed efforts to revive their father. The daughter pulled at her hair and screamed words of denial as her own tears spilled in an endless river. The boy wasn't screaming, but his face was streaked with tears as well. He was blubbering and urging his mother to "bring him back, please bring him back" over and over.

After spending quite a few years divorcing himself from entanglements of any kind with other human beings and avoiding extremes of emotion in general, Harlan's instinct was to turn away from their pain. As a man who'd known sudden, shocking loss, he empathized with the mother and her children. He remembered exactly how that felt, and just thinking about the night he received the news of his parents' accident brought a rare welling of tears to his eyes. Before the mist could turn into a waterfall, he clamped down on the memories and forced himself to focus on the moment at hand. There could be no turning away from the tragedy of this family's loss. Instinct to the contrary be damned. What was happening here wasn't just happening to them, though they'd taken the brunt of it thus far. For the sake of everyone present, the situation had to be faced head-on, with fortitude and resolve, otherwise they were all likely to meet the same fate as the fallen patriarch.

Harlan stood up and straightened his tie, fiddling frustratedly with the knot for a moment. He was not a fan of the bloody things and could never get them to hang just right. While he was messing about with it—a thing he recognized as a delaying tactic, even as it was happening—Bradley sidled up closer to him again and spoke in a hushed whisper.

"Harlan, we really need to talk."

Harlan nodded. "Yes, we do. About all manner of things, but I suspect you won't be happy with anything I have to say. It's time the secrets of the past were brought into the light. Perhaps if we'd confronted the horror of it all when we were young, none of this would be happening now."

Bradley put a trembling hand on his shoulder. "But—"

Harlan sneered, brushing the hand away. "Fuck off, you simpering coward." He turned his head and glared defiantly at the other man. "Lest we forget, it might never have happened at all if not for the staggering stupidity of you and your pathetic sidekick."

Bradley winced. He looked chastened and desperate, on the brink of tears. Harlan gave not a single damn. Rebuking the former homecoming king contender felt liberating. He felt freer in his mind than he'd felt in a long, long time, and he looked forward to feeling even freer soon. Soon he would shrug off the burdens of the past forever.

First, though, there were things in the here and now that needed confronting.

Harlan ceased fiddling with his tie and crossed the room to stand with the grieving family. As he arrived, the widow was attempting to turn her husband's corpse onto its back. What she thought she might accomplish by doing that was unclear. The body was still slumped across the table, the surface of which was awash with large splashes of crimson. Because the man's head was hanging over the edge of the table, a great deal more of his blood had pattered on the floor below. The woman's face was turning red again from the strain of trying to flip the body over.

Harlan cleared his throat. "Madam, I think you should stop."

The woman ignored him as she continued working at her sad task. By then she had the body turned onto its side. Grunting from the effort, she gave it another big heave. The body flipped over as she intended. Unfortunately, however, the amount of exertion she'd put into the effort created too much momentum. The body kept going and slid off the side of the table, landing with a heavy thump on the floor a moment later.

The teenage daughter screamed and threw herself into her trembling brother's arms.

The widow sighed and stared blankly for a moment at her husband's unmoving body. Then she resumed crying. Harlan watched her and wondered how long he should wait before initiating the necessary questioning. She surprised him, however, when she took her hand away from her face and looked him right in the eye, righteous fury infusing her grief as she spat out her next words: *"Who the fuck did this to my husband!?"*

Harlan flinched slightly in the face of her rage, but he did not back away, holding fast to his resolve to begin the difficult work of sorting things out. "I'd like to know the answer to that myself, ma'am. Do you remember—"

She abruptly spun away from him and glared at the Martinson sisters, who were still seated at their table. "It was one of you bitches, wasn't it?" She snatched a steak knife from the table in front of her. The same knife she'd waved at Harlan a few minutes earlier, only now it was stained with her husband's blood. "Yeah, of course it was." She advanced a few steps in the direction of the sisters, sneering menacingly as she waved the knife around again. "You were the ones antagonizing him. Belittling him in front of his kids with your bullshit insinuations." She was still slowly advancing on the sisters as she said these things, but they gave no outward signs of being intimidated. "One of you got up when the lights went out and fucking did this. Admit it."

The sisters exchanged amused expressions.

Then they burst out laughing.

Nina smirked. "Honey, if I'd iced that tubby cuckold of yours, I'd tell you." She flipped a hand around. "In this situation . . . and this setting . . . why not? I'd absolutely admit it. Hell, I'd be proud of it. And you know something else? He wouldn't be the first man I've killed. Far from it. It's kind of a hobby of mine, actually."

"Mine, too," Tina put in.

Nina nodded. "Yes, we both very much enjoy a good stabbing now and then. It's good fun. That's the truth. But right now, lady, you're the only one with a bloody knife in your hand."

Breath hissed through the widow's teeth as she strove to keep her anger from boiling over. "Exactly what the fuck are you trying to say?"

Nina stood up from her chair, backed away from the table, and did a slow turn in her heels, allowing all watching a long, unimpeded look at every inch of her body. She smiled when she stood facing the furious widow again. "See? Not a drop of blood on me."

Tina followed her sister's lead and did a slow turn of her own, ending with a wink directed at the widow. "Yeah. Me either. No blood. No fucking knife. Nothing but sheer hotness."

The sisters high-fived at this remark.

Nina sat down again, striking an unconcerned pose as she turned sideways a bit and crossed her long, shapely legs. She smiled. "But you, you don't just have a weapon, you've got blood all over you. You look like a gore geyser hit you right in the chest." She giggled. Then she snapped her fingers. "But, wait, there's more!"

Now it was Tina who giggled as she sat down.

Still staring unflinchingly at the widow, Nina raised an eyebrow. "You were right there with him. Nobody had a better opportunity than you. You did it. You killed him. As for motive, I'm thinking it's because my wild guess about your extramarital activities was bang on the money. Maybe you didn't plan to kill him, but when the lights went out, you seized the moment and did the little porker in. All so you wouldn't have to face his eventual questions about the dubious parentage of your whiny little brats."

The widow's hand repeatedly clenched and unclenched around the handle of the knife. "How dare you. I didn't kill my husband, but I fucking well ought to kill you for even *suggesting* such a thing."

To Harlan, it sure sounded like she meant it. Maybe murder wasn't the kind of thing she'd ever normally consider, but in moments of extreme distress, people were often capable of things they wouldn't normally do. In that way, Nina Martinson had an actual point, cruel cattiness aside. He didn't believe this woman had actually murdered her husband. Not a chance. Her grief was too real. If she could fake that level of feeling that believably, she belonged in motion pictures. He was considering how he might intervene and cool the temperature in the room when the teenage daughter shrugged out of her brother's embrace and pointed to something under the table.

"What is that?"

Harlan followed her pointing finger and frowned when he spied the crumpled scrap of red velvet. He moved closer to the table and bent to retrieve it, groaning at the creaking of his knees when he stood again. Still frowning, he held it up between pinched thumb and forefinger and turned slowly about so everyone could see the item for what it was.

A red Christmas stocking with a white cuff. Written in glued-on glitter on the cuff was the name Alan.

Only now there was a black X through his name.

SIXTEEN

CONTRARY TO WHAT THE HOODED man said during his closed-circuit broadcast, no one came for Alexandra Harcourt when the countdown clock on the screen reached 0:00. Nor did the door to her room automatically unlock. After several minutes, the white numerals on the screen disappeared and the snowy static returned. The buzz issuing from the speaker became annoying after a short time, prompting her to rise from her seated position against the foot of the bed. She approached the TV and used a knob to lower the volume without silencing it entirely. On the off-chance another broadcast began, she wanted to be able to hear it.

The chain links clinked and rattled as she went to the door again to test the lock. Once again, it did not budge to any amount of pressure. In light of her previous experience, this did not come as a surprise, but she felt disappointment anyway. Not for the first time, she wondered if any of what the hooded man said during his speech was true.

Maybe there were no other guests, nor any formal dinner party. She figured it was just as likely all those things were fictional, all a part of an elaborate scheme to mess with her head. A form of psychological torture not dissimilar to what captured spies were made to endure at the hands of an enemy determined to break them down. What there was to gain by making her believe she was in a house filled with people in a similar predicament, she had no idea. She wasn't carrying around a head full of valuable secrets. She was just an ordinary person trapped in an extraordinarily bizarre situation, one without an obvious way out.

Giving up on the door, she crossed back to the other side of the room and once again stared out the window at the rear grounds of the property. Because it was dark, there wasn't much to see other than lazily drifting snowflakes, and she almost turned away again after just a few seconds. Then she caught a glimpse of flickering light in the vicinity of the garden. There and gone in the space of little more than a second, but it was soon replaced by two fainter points of light. The little orange specks occasionally moved and it wasn't long before she realized what she was seeing. At least two people were out there smoking. She considered banging on the thick window pane to get their attention, but she quickly thought better of it. Drawing the attention of people who lived or worked here probably wasn't the best idea, given that they were almost certainly complicit in whatever was being done to her. It was the same reason she hadn't bothered banging on the door or calling out for help earlier.

There was no one to help her here.

She was on her own.

She continued observing the specks of light, however, and after a while her eyes adjusted and she was better able to discern the shape of things down there in the garden. The cigarette smokers were standing on a narrow concrete walkway between rows of hedges. One of the tiny points of orange light went out but was soon replaced. If the smokers were conversing, their voices were too faint to hear. Unless they started shouting, she doubted she'd be able to hear them through the thick pane of glass anyway. Not having anything else to do, however, she kept on watching them a short while longer.

Until she heard a low, anguished voice speak somewhere behind her. She let out a startled gasp and whirled about, putting her naked back against the cold window. A reflexive shiver of intense fear sent chills rippling through her as she braced herself to again face the menacing hooded figure. She needed a few seconds to realize no one was with her in the room. Of course not. Even distracted, she would have heard the rattle of a key in the lock or the creaking of hinges as the door swung inward.

Then she heard the anguished voice again.

She belatedly noticed the field of snowy static no longer filled the

TV screen. In its place was an image of a familiar-looking man sitting naked in a chair in a shadowy room. She frowned and moved closer to the TV, gasping in surprise when she finally recognized him. It was Stephen Bain. Her old stalker. The man who'd made her life a living hell for a while. Spooked by the prospect of legal consequences for his behavior, he'd slinked out of her life, seemingly forever, only now he was back. A wave of anger swept over Alexandra as she glared at the low-def image of Bain's hated face. *Of course* the son of a bitch was behind her abduction. All these years, he'd been biding his time, only pretending to live the upstanding life of a reformed person, all the while putting together the perfect plan to finally have what he really wanted.

Me, she thought bitterly. *He never let go of his fucking obsession.*

The anger directed at Bain was sheer reflex. She needed a few a moments to push through the residual effects of her old trauma before she could begin to see what was really happening. Or at least what *appeared* to be happening. The man in the chair was definitely Bain. He looked a little older—it'd been over a decade, after all—but otherwise his appearance wasn't much changed. Even his hair style was exactly as she remembered, short but with that little hank of longer hair hanging rakishly across his forehead.

He was tied to the chair and was exhibiting what appeared to be a high level of distress. There was a bruise under his left eye. His bottom lip was split open and leaking blood. Tears spilled from his eyes and a sheen of sweat covered his skin. He whimpered softly and intermittently whispered tearful pleas for mercy. Once he cried out for someone named Natalie in a particularly pitiful way. From her years of keeping social media tabs on him, Alexandra recognized this as the name of the woman he'd married several years ago.

Bain alternated between staring at the lens of the camera in front of him and tracking the occasional movements of a dark-clad other person in the room. Because of the camera angle, Alexandra only got occasional glimpses of the lower half of the other person's body. It was a shirtless person wearing black pants and black gloves. She glimpsed just enough of the lower portion of the person's torso to deduce it most likely belonged to a somewhat flabby man. The mystery person was busy moving apparently heavy items around in what seemed like a small, cluttered room. Most of the low level of light in the room was focused on Bain's face, which made it impossible to clearly see what the other man was doing.

Then the sounds of movement stopped.

A dark form was standing directly behind Bain, presumably the same person now fully cloaked in shadow. Bain turned his head as far as his tight bonds would allow, which was not far. The muscles in his neck stood out in stark relief from the strain. He was shivering in terror as he started pleading with the person behind him. "P-please don't hurt me. Please." He sniffled and sucked in a reedy breath before continuing. "Why are you doing this to me? I haven't fucking *done* anything."

Alexandra grunted.

Maybe not in recent history, Stephen.

"Face the camera," a guttural voice intoned.

Bain still had his head turned to the side, straining to see the person behind him. "Come on, goddammit! You've *got* to listen to me! I've got a wife and kid. They'll be fucking lost without me." He grunted loudly and tried twisting against his bonds to no avail. "Fine. If pleas to your humanity aren't going to work, I'll do anything. You want money? I'll give you every penny I have. Want me to suck your dick? I'll do that, too. Just *tell* me, goddammit!"

A brief silence ensued.

Then the same guttural voice said, "Face the camera."

Bain sighed and finally faced forward, resignation evident in his expression as his shoulders sagged. "There. I'm facing the fucking camera. Will you finally tell me what you want from—"

Alexandra shrieked as a heavy blade crashed down through the crown of Bain's skull and cleaved his head straight down the middle all the way to his neck.

SEVENTEEN

THE WIDOW SNATCHED THE STOCKING out of Harlan's grasp and stared at it wide-eyed as she held it close to her face. The look on her face registered confusion and distress along with a strong dose of wild incomprehension. She looked like someone who'd stumbled upon an artifact left behind by ancient aliens, a thing utterly beyond her capacity to understand.

"There's something inside it."

That was the daughter speaking, pointing again.

Colette had risen from her table and crept a bit closer, drawn both by morbid curiosity and an interest in learning anything that might help her better understand what was happening. Things were undeniably weird at Raven's Reach, but she wasn't convinced this latest twist was evidence of sinister intent on the part of their mysterious host. Her thinking at that point wasn't far removed from the theory posited by Nina Martinson. The wife was the one with blood all over her. She had a knife. The idea that she'd abruptly decided to kill her husband during the brief power outage didn't strike her as so farfetched, not with George's corpse currently cooling under the bed in her room.

The widow frowned as she gave the stocking a shake. "Doesn't feel like it, honey."

The daughter made an exasperated sound. "There *is*, Mom," she said in a whiny voice. "Check the bottom."

Colette squinted as she crept a little closer. Then she saw it. A barely perceptible bulge at the very bottom of the stocking. The object, whatever it was, must be almost weightless. It might easily have gone unnoticed altogether, if not for the extra-observant child.

Still frowning, the widow reached into the stocking and felt around until her fingers closed on the object. She did not immediately withdraw the item, but her face registered an even deeper level of confusion as her fingers rubbed over its surface. At last, she slowly withdrew the object and held it up for everyone to see. By then, everyone was up and edging closer for a better look, even the Martinson sisters.

There was a period of stupefied silence.

Then Nina Martinson clapped a hand over her mouth and giggled. "Oh my god!"

Her sister also laughed. "Holy shit. It's a lump of fucking coal. Lady, your husband has officially had the worst Christmas in recorded history. He got stabbed to fucking death by his wife and got a lump of coal from Santa. That is fucking *epic!*"

Colette couldn't suppress a small sputter of laughter. It was inappropriate and normally she would be mortified by accidentally expressing mirth in the face of something so tragic. Not because she actually cared about the feelings of the bereaved. God, no. In general, she couldn't care less about the terrible things that befell other people, especially lower-class people like this family, who barely even counted as real people in her opinion. However, openly laughing at them in front of witnesses was widely viewed as not a classy thing to do. Fortunately, perhaps because the Martinson sisters' shameless mockery was so over-the-top, no one appeared to notice her own outburst. Then she saw Bradley Winthorpe giving her a reproving look and realized that wasn't exactly true. The mild embarrassment she felt gave way to anger. How dare the man. The fucking *hypocrite*. He of all people was in no position to pass moral judgment on anyone. Or . . . wait.

Maybe this wasn't a reproving look at all. The longer she looked at him, the more she perceived a beseeching quality to his expression. There was something he was trying to project silently and with more than a touch of desperation, his facial features shifting and twitching in ways that verged on comical, as if he was hoping she could read his mind. Upon realizing this, her angry glare gave way to a confused frown. She shook her head to indicate her lack of understanding. He jerked his head to one side and rolled his eyes about in a way she interpreted as meaning he wanted to have a private talk with her away from the rest of them.

Interesting.

He was probably shitting himself over Harlan's interrupted revelation of secrets, which was not surprising. Of all of them, he was most culpable in what happened on that long ago night. Well, he and his best friend, Jacob Martinelli, whose absence here tonight struck her as an odd omission.

Colette mouthed the word "later", which clearly frustrated Bradley, judging from the look on his face. She didn't care, though. The widow had resumed bickering with the Martinson sisters and for the time being their heated exchange was of far greater interest than whatever pathetic pleading Bradley had in mind. The sisters were giggling again, undoubtedly having made yet another of their patented scathing remarks. Meanwhile, the widow's face was flushed so red with rage it looked like an overripe tomato, ready to burst at any moment. It almost seemed as if the sisters were deliberately trying to goad her into taking a run at them with that knife.

Maybe they were.

She surprised herself with an abrupt and unplanned interjection. "Excuse me?"

Despite the attempted interruption, the widow and the sisters remained locked in their stare down, the air in the room crackling with tension as all eyes remained focused on them. Well, *almost* all eyes. Bradley was again trying to snag her attention.

She ignored him as she loudly cleared her throat and raised her voice. "Excuse me?"

Things remained as they were a beat longer. Then, slowly, one by one, each person present turned toward her. She laughed in a nervous way as she surveyed their expectant expressions. "Oh, good. Thank you all for acknowledging my existence. I know we all have a lot we're dealing with right now." Her eyes slid briefly toward the glowering widow. "Some more than others, obviously." She coughed. "But . . . is it just me, or is it a little weird how these two . . ." She hooked a thumb in the direction of the Martinson sisters. ". . . have basically confessed to being a serial-killing team, and we've all just decided to ignore it." She turned fully toward the sisters now. "Or was that all just a morbid joke?"

Nina shook her head. "Oh, no. That was for real."

Tina nodded. "Yah. One hundred percent not a joke. Hell, it's the whole reason we're here tonight. I mean, aside from our role in what happened to that fucking retard way back when. Obviously."

"What are you saying?" Harlan Ross asked them.

Tina shrugged. "We're being blackmailed. Do you think we *wanted* to come to this godforsaken place? God, no. But we had no choice. Whoever put this whole thing together has evidence of our crimes. The kind that can't be faked or denied. We were threatened with exposure if we didn't come."

A silence descended as everyone else took a moment to digest this information.

"You kill people. Murder them." Harlan again, speaking in a calm, deliberate tone that still managed to sound appalled. "I just want to get this straight. You do it for fun. For kicks. Not out of some sense of righteous retribution? They're not pedos or violent abusers?"

Nina gave him the frowning look of someone who felt unfairly put-upon. "I mean, *maybe* some of them are, who knows. You kill enough people—and we've killed a bunch—odds are at least one or two of them aren't saints, but that's definitely not why we do it."

Tina nodded. "It's a personal fulfillment thing. Sisterly bonding."

Harlan shook his head. "Unbelievable. Absolutely un-fucking-believable."

Nina groaned. "Oh, come on. Don't be like that. We're friends. You're not gonna hold this against us, are you?"

Harlan laughed, a sound filled with weariness. "I don't even know how to answer that question. We were friends once, it's true. Good friends, even. But you have no heart. No conscience, no soul. You're psychopaths."

Nina harrumphed. "Gosh. You make it sound like a bad thing."

Harlan made an exasperated sound. "It *is*."

Colette hadn't fully believed the sisters' story about being serial killers, but now she was convinced. Oddly enough, however, she felt more relief than fear. If, somehow, she survived the night and managed to escape this place, she was confident she could successfully pin the blame for George's violent death on someone else. Looking around, she realized there was no shortage of viable alternate suspects present, as well as more who weren't even in the room. Those creepy hooded servants were still around somewhere. Mix in a generous amount of chaos and general confusion and the stage was set for getting away with virtually anything.

The widow started laughing in a genuinely amused way that didn't quite mirror the affected schoolgirl giggles of the Martinson sisters, but which wasn't that far off, either. She sounded more unhinged than before. Noticing the bloody knife still clutched tightly in her hand, Colette backed off a few steps. The woman was under a lot of strain. Maybe she'd killed her husband and maybe she hadn't. Either way, she might snap from the stress of it all at any second, possibly in a violent way. If she *had* killed him, well, she was every bit as dangerous as the loony sisters.

Nina looked at her. "What's so funny, bitch?"

The widow slowly brought her laughter under control. "You. You're funny. You're *all* funny. Also, I'm just tired of keeping up the pretense."

She turned away from them and jabbed the steak knife into Harlan's abdomen. Three times in quick succession, like a felon shanking a fellow prisoner. She left the blade embedded in his belly as she walked away, laughing again at the startled gasps and shocked expressions on the faces of the other guests.

With the exception, that is, of her son and daughter, who were now following her away from the circle of tables toward the closed roll door. The teenagers were no longer crying and wailing. There were smirks on their faces as they filed past their father.

The roll door loudly ratcheted upward, revealing a line of hooded servants standing out in the hallway. They stood there silently, waiting to block the exit of anyone other than the mother and her kids. Once the now fatherless family had moved beyond them and were out of sight, one of the servants stepped forward, tossed something into the room, and lowered the door again.

Inside the dining hall, there was a long moment of stunned silence. Then Harlan Ross dropped to his knees and groaned.

Nina Martinson grunted. "Huh. Have to admit, I did not see that coming."

EIGHTEEN

IN THE HALLWAY OUTSIDE THE dining hall, the woman formerly posing as Sandra Dozier—a person who never actually existed—was met by the woman in the red catsuit, who at present was not wearing her hood. This woman's name was Janine Blankenship. She was pretty and had medium-length black hair in a bob cut.

Janine smiled hesitantly and said, "Deviating from the script, Ms. Thornton?"

Eileen Thornton scowled as she peeled the blond wig off her head and agitatedly thrust it into the hands of her startled assistant. "Obviously." She snapped the back of a hand across Janine's face, eliciting a yelp. "Don't state obvious things, girl. You're smarter than that."

Janine nodded, wincing as she gingerly touched the spot on her face scratched by Eileeen's phony wedding ring. "Yes, ma'am. Sorry."

"Don't apologize, either. What's done is done."

Janine looked on the verge of reflexively apologizing again, but hit the mental brakes before that could happen. She nodded. "Yes, ma'am."

Eileen removed a skull cap from her head, revealing her own natural darker shade. These longer locks were being kept in place by numerous bobby pins. She began pinching them out and dropping them on the floor. "What's happening with Alex?"

Janine again smiled in a hesitant way. A frequent target of her employer's penchant for physical abuse, she felt perpetually gun-shy about being struck again. She tolerated it for a few reasons, one being that the abuse rarely ever progressed beyond the occasional random smack.

But mostly it was about the money.

On paper, she was an unaccomplished college dropout with an undistinguished work history, the work she did as Eileen's top assistant not being the sort she could ever put on a resume. Her handsome salary was dispersed among a variety of offshore accounts untouchable by the government. Despite being rich, she lived in a modest apartment in the town of Thornton and drove a ten-year-old used Acura. As far as her disapproving family was concerned, she was a destitute loser constantly in need of handouts. Handouts she always accepted because she hated her smug parents and it amused her to take money she didn't actually need. Eileen's other employees all had similar stories. She recruited the vulnerable and purchased their loyalty. No one ever betrayed that loyalty because they rightfully feared the consequences of doing so. Also, while the other assistants did not earn as much as Janine, they all made significantly more money than they could ever make in a regular job.

"We showed Alex the tape of Stephen Bain's execution. It seemed to have the desired effect. I believe she'll be susceptible to suggestion of virtually any kind at this point."

Eileen plucked out the last of the bobby pins and allowed it to slip from her fingers as she shook out her long locks. "Excellent. No indication at all she was ever close to realizing who Bain actually was?"

Janine shook her head. "No, ma'am. Looked to me like she really believed she was watching the murder of an old adversary." She chuckled. "Bain even referenced her real name at one point and it didn't seem to trigger anything."

Eileen laughed. "Fantastic. I'll drop in on her soon. Meanwhile, I need to go have a word with Trog."

"Trog" was what Eileen called her weird pervert brother. It was short for troglodyte.

"Yes, ma'am."

Eileen started moving past her. "I'll be back within the hour, hopefully sooner."

She was three steps beyond where Janine was standing when the struggling actor hired to play Sandra Dozier's teenaged son called out to her. "Hey, hold up a sec. I need a word with you, lady."

Eileen froze in place for a moment, her back to Janine and the others.

Janine winced as she preemptively moved out of the way. Something unpleasant was about to happen. One look at her employer's stiff posture was enough to confirm this.

Another silent beat passed.

When Eileen finally turned around, a falsely radiant smile was plastered to her face. Janine had worked with Eileen Thornton long enough to plainly see the madness lurking behind the expression. Unfortunately for this dumb kid—who was actually in his twenties rather than his teens—all he saw was the smile.

The expression stayed on her face as she came a step closer. "Yes, Jonathan?"

That was the actor's actual name. Jonathan Acker.

The girl who'd played his sister shrank back a step or two upon getting a look at Eileen's face. Her real name was Marnie Richardson. Marnie had appeared in a few off-off-Broadway stage productions of obscure, experimental plays. Apparently, she was better at reading people than her dumbass male counterpart. Not that it was likely to save her.

Acker was sneering as he said, "Look, I just want to be sure we get paid the full agreed-on amount. We rehearsed a lot more shit than that. I spent weeks memorizing a bunch of dialogue I apparently didn't need to learn after all, because for some fucking reason, you decided to cut it all short."

Still smiling, Eileen came another step closer. Her eyelids were fluttering more rapidly now, which Janine recognized as not a good sign for Acker, who was still being awfully slow in recognizing his misstep. Janine wished she could slap the guy. He wasn't a bad dude, but he suffered from a touch of willful arrogance she'd warned him wouldn't fly in this setting. She felt bad for him, but he should've taken her warnings to heart.

Eileen laughed. "Not that I owe you an explanation, child, but here it is anyway. I cut things short because the jig was about up. I didn't expect Nina Martinson to guess you weren't actually that man's children. Once that happened, it was only a matter of time until the whole thing unraveled. Even using the most sophisticated techniques, as we do here, reprogramming a human being's mind is a delicate thing. Apply the wrong pressures and it all comes apart. I could see that was about to happen and no longer wanted to continue with the

Dozier family scenario. From the start, you were told this was all subject to my whim. That I might opt to abort at any point."

Acker did not appear mollified by any of this. "That might make sense if we were talking about anyone other than Alan Dozier. That fucking guy's as oblivious as a brick wall. We could've kept going with it. I just think—"

"Enough!"

This time Eileen's tone was laced with enough obvious venom to finally silence the indignant actor, though the tight-lipped look on his face suggested he might not remain quiet for long. Janine wished she had the ability to send messages telepathically. If she could, she'd definitely be telling this headstrong idiot it was time to shift to ass-kissing deferential mode.

Eileen approached Acker until they were standing face-to-face. "Your attitude is unfortunate. You seem to think we're on equal footing. That this is just another gig and I'm just another eccentric director. You are sadly mistaken on both counts."

She put a hand out with her palm turned up.

In another moment, one of the black-hooded servants stepped forward and put a gun in it.

Acker's face blanched when he saw the gun. His eyes widened and he held his hands up in a pleading gesture as he backed up a step. "Hey, come on, I meant no offense. I was just really into the role, but I get now that I overstepped my bounds, okay? I'm really fucking sorry."

Eileen smiled. "Apology not accepted."

She raised the gun and fired a round into Acker's forehead. Marnie Richardson yelped as her colleague's blood and brains spattered her face and the front of her blouse. Eileen sneered and shook her head as the actor's corpse dropped to the floor. She held her hand out again and the same black-hooded servant reclaimed his weapon.

Marnie was mewling pitifully in a way that was not exactly unexpected given the circumstances. She had not anticipated seeing a close co-worker murdered right in front of her and was understandably experiencing a significant level of shock. The girl was not a purely innocent soul, of course. Like Acker, she'd been fully apprised of all the potential variables inherent in the gig. She went into it knowing Alan Dozier was likely to be killed at some point during the evening's festivities. It might happen at an early point or a later one depending on how the night evolved, but it was all but certain to happen sooner or later.

She'd also known there was a strong likelihood other guests might also perish. All of that, however, she'd managed to compartmentalize as just being part of the job. In her mind, up until now, the guests were other actors and any blood that might be spilled was just special effects. The promise of an unusually hefty payday along with the challenge of doing improvisational acting in a truly one-of-a-kind setting made the highly questionable morality of it all worth it as far as she was concerned. Janine knew this because Marnie had told her so several times, often when they were in bed together.

Eileen glanced at her top assistant. "Dispose of the dead one in the usual way." Her gaze shifted to Marnie, lingering on her a moment. "Put that one in one of the cells under the house. I'll figure out what to do with her later."

Janine nodded, flipping her boss a little military-style salute. "Will do."

Marnie wailed in despair. "*No!* I didn't do anything wrong! I did everything you asked of me."

Eileen grunted. "Which is why you're being slapped in a cell instead of bleeding out on the floor like this idiot." She indicated Acker with a contemptuous lift of her chin. "You might want to stop whining before I change my mind about that."

Marnie continued whimpering but evidently had nothing further to say. She directed a pleading look at Janine.

Janine shook her head.

She felt no sentimentality where this girl was concerned. The actors were always just as disposable as the guests. She didn't mind having fun with them whenever the opportunity arose, but it was best not to get attached.

"I'm off to see Trog," Eileen said, glancing again at Janine. "We reconvene here within the hour."

Janine nodded, but her boss didn't see the gesture because, by then, she was already striding rapidly away in the other direction.

NINETEEN

"WAS THAT A GUNSHOT?"

Following the departure of the widow and her two children, the Martinson sisters were the first to come to Harlan. They each took him by an arm and helped him up off his knees and into a chair pulled away from one of the tables. He groaned and grimaced at each little movement, gasping loudest when he was plopped into the chair.

The bottom half of his shirt was stained red on one side. His face was sheened with sweat and his cheeks flushed red. The way his head slowly wobbled about was clear evidence of wooziness. He started mumbling the same question about the gunshot again, but Nina ignored this as she went about the work of removing his tie and undoing the buttons of his shirt. He cried out as she tugged the stained side of his shirt free of his pants and pulled it gently away from his wounded flesh.

Standing nearby, her sister gnawed on a thumbnail, chipping the red polish as she watched Nina tend to the man. "How's it looking?"

Nina shrugged. "I'm sure it hurts like hell, but I don't think we're looking at anything fatal here. We're talking about a short blade used on a thick body. He needs professional medical attention to err on the safe side, though."

Tina nodded. "That's the real dilemma, isn't it? We're trapped in this fucking place. For now, anyway. Getting him to a hospital might not be doable for a while."

"All the more reason to figure some way out of this mess," Nina said, twisting her head about while she remained kneeling in front of Harlan. She sighed at the sight of the closed doors. "We're gonna have to smash our way out of here, aren't we?"

Harlan laughed woozily, then winced again as Nina pressed two more of the thick formal dinner napkins against his wounded abdomen. "Anyone have a battering ram handy? Nina Dina says we need to smash our way out."

Nina frowned. "What did you call me?"

"Nina Dina." This time he said it in a sing-song way. "Nina Dina Banina Farina. Hey, you know who was a pretty good actor? Dennis fucking Farina, that's who."

Tina chortled. "He's feeling a little goofy."

Nina sighed. "Blood loss and physical trauma will sometimes do that to a person. We've seen that often enough doing our thing."

"Why are you helping him?"

Nina glanced up upon hearing Colette Hammerschmidt's voice. She and Bradley Winthorpe had returned from their expedition to the bar at the rear of the dining hall. In her hands were two dark-colored bottles of wine, a pair of glittering wine glasses, and a corkscrew. Bradley came bearing three bottles of bourbon and a single whiskey glass.

Nina frowned. "Planning on getting fucked up, are we?"

Colette shrugged. "Why not? We're being held prisoner without any obvious means of escape. Drunken oblivion is as valid a reaction to the circumstances as any other." She set the wine bottles on the table nearest to where Nina was administering to Ross and began the process of opening one with the corkscrew. "Now I'll ask you again—why are you helping a man who, just a short while ago, explained in no uncertain terms why he considers both of you subhuman garbage?"

The sisters exchanged a glance.

Tina shrugged. "It's not that complicated. Yes, he said some mean things, but he's still our Harley. We love him."

Colette had the cork halfway out of the bottle when she paused in the act of removing it and glanced at Tina with a raised eyebrow. "Are you being serious right now?"

Tina nodded. "Of course. Why would you think otherwise?"

Colette laughed and resumed twisting the corkscrew. The cork came loose with a loud pop seconds later. She poured red wine into one of the glasses and raised it, holding it daintily by the stem. After taking a first tentative sip, she looked at Tina and said, "Why? Because none of us have seen each other in twenty years. Right? Have there been any partial reunions of the old gang in the interim of which I've been unaware? Please say no. I don't know if my fragile ego could take the thought of being snubbed."

She tittered as she took another drink.

Tina shook her head. "If there have been any reunions, we haven't been a part of them."

Bradley laughed in a bitterly derisive way. "Of course there haven't been any fucking reunions, Colette." He took a swig straight from one of the bourbon bottles and grimaced as the booze slid down his throat. The other bottles he'd set on the table next to Colette's spare bottle of wine, along with the whiskey glass he'd evidently decided not to use. "It was part of our vow, remember? After graduation, we were never going to see each other again. It was for the best, we said. The only way to guarantee our secrets would stay secret. Because we wouldn't have to look at each other and feel the weight of that guilt." He chuckled, shaking his head. "Stupid teenage logic. Full confession, though. I stayed in touch with Jake off and on through our twenties."

Tina tilted her head, frowning in surprise. "You did?"

Bradley took another big slug of bourbon. "Yep. We were best friends. Out of all of us, he dealt with the guilt of it the worst. He reached out to me when he was struggling several times and I tried my damnedest to help him through it, but after a while it became too fucking much to deal with. He became a full-blown alcoholic and drug addict. Just utterly helpless and hopeless. His troubles were holding me back and I wanted to get on with my life."

Tina grunted. "So you cut him loose?"

Bradley scowled. "You're goddamn right I did."

Colette sighed heavily. "The point, my dear old friends, is I don't understand how these two . . ." She nodded at the sisters. ". . . can claim to love a person they haven't seen in decades. My God, we were all still children back then, really. Different people entirely. It just strikes me as a dubious notion. Put generously."

She smiled again as she took her biggest drink yet.

Tina rolled her eyes. "Give me a break with the smugly superior attitude. I'm being totally serious here. We do love Harley. Same as we've always loved all of you. Doesn't matter if we haven't seen each other in one year or ten or twenty. The feeling's still there. It never goes away. Isn't that right, sis?"

Still on her knees in front of Harlan, Nina glanced at her sister. "That's right."

Colette sputtered disbelieving laughter and downed the last of her first glass of wine.

Bradley snorted.

He moved away from them a moment and retrieved the item one of the hooded servants had tossed into the dining hall before closing and locking the roll door a second time. Another stocking. This one had the name JAKE written in glued-on glitter letters on the cuff. Like the stocking associated with the dead man on the floor, it was marked through with a black X. Unlike that other stocking, the bottom of this one sagged more noticeably, filled with multiple large lumps of coal.

He came back toward them and held the stocking up. "This means he's dead, right? My old friend?"

Colette's expression sobered somewhat as she glanced at the stocking. "Fair assumption. I imagine we would've seen him here tonight otherwise."

Bradley sighed. "Fuck."

He sniffled and wiped away a slow-rolling tear.

"Having regrets, are we? Wish we'd done more to help instead of being a self-centered bastard?"

Bradley's expression sharpened as his head snapped toward her. "Fuck you. You've always been a stuck-up bitch. That's one thing that's never changed."

On impulse, he wound up and threw the stocking at her, and she had to lean slightly to one side as it went fluttering by. She met Bradley's livid gaze and laughed before turning her head and showing Tina a raised eyebrow. "Not feeling the love from this direction, I'm afraid. Your premise of undying love and loyalty doesn't strike me as well-founded as you'd like to believe."

Tina shrugged. "What the rest of you feel is on you. Question our sincerity all you like, but I'm not lying. My sister and I love Harlan. We love the rest of you. Believe it or don't. I'm done arguing with you about it."

Colette was in the process of gulping more wine as Tina said this. Some flew from her mouth as she sputtered laughter again. "Oh, that's it, eh? We're done with the discussion because you say so?"

Tina's expression hardened. "Yes."

Colette smirked. "Nonsense. You and your sister are serial killers. Unless you're lying about that, and I don't think you are, that means you willfully stalk and kill other human beings. I have to presume you do this because you enjoy it. Am I wrong?"

Tina shook her head. "You are not."

Colette's features shifted, becoming imbued with a level of genuine curiosity that, for the moment at least, almost entirely displaced her usual sneering cynicism. "So how do you reconcile this solemn and abiding love you say you have for us with the pleasure you derive from torturing and murdering innocent people?"

This time it was Nina who answered. Her hands were stained with Harlan's blood as she finally got to her feet and turned toward the other woman. "It's easier than you think. In our normal lives we present as normal people, because in that life we *are* normal people. Normal feelings, normal interests, and ordinary jobs. Ordinary everything, basically. When we go on the hunt and kill, we access other versions of ourselves. Hidden versions. In effect, we become—"

"Different people," Tina finished for her.

Colette stared thoughtfully at them a moment, brow still furrowed. Then she shivered and said, "Dear God, that is absolutely chilling."

Nina shrugged. "It is what it is. Most successful serial killers, the ones who operate without getting caught for decades, are the same way."

Still holding her wine glass loosely by the stem, Colette observed the sisters with narrowed eyes, not noticing the wine in the glass was close to spilling over the brim. "I imagine what happened senior year must have acted as a kind of triggering event for you two," she said, apparently not yet ready to drop the subject of the sisters' career in recreational murder. "I've often heard it said that people like yourselves wind up doing the vile things they do because of youthful trauma. Am I right?"

Tina looked at her. "No."

Colette looked surprised. "No?"

Tina shook her head. "Not in this case. Not exactly. I mean, I guess there was trauma of a sort, but it was nothing to do with senior year. For me, it goes back a couple years earlier."

She spent a few minutes describing the day she came home from school early and spied on her mother fucking the neighbor kid.

Colette's features shifted again, conveying skepticism. "Are you kidding me? *That* was your triggering event? Your mother getting it on with some young stud on the sly?" She shook her head, snorting in disbelief. A bit of wine finally slopped over the brim of the glass and she appeared not to notice as the droplets pattered on the floor. "I get that it was upsetting given your age at the time, but how could something so mundane send you down such a dark path?"

"It taught me that everything I thought was good and true and pure in life was a lie," Tina said, her matter-of-fact tone belying her words. "Therefore, life itself had no meaning."

"And to be fair," Nina put in, nose crinkling as she thought about it, "I was just following my sister's lead. It started with her, but it never really bothered me. The killing, I mean. It was just a really different way to have fun."

"You're a sociopath," Bradley said, scowling after yet another straight-from-the-bottle slug of bourbon. "Both of you. No conscience."

Tina rolled her eyes. "Thanks for the input. Very insightful. Can we move on from the fucking psychoanalysis? We're still stuck in a deeply fucked-up situation. We should be brainstorming ways out of it."

Nina nodded. "Totally. Harlan might have been loopy when he said it, but that *did* sound like a gunshot from the hallway. We need to focus on the threat we're facing, because it's not just gonna go away."

Bradley barked spiteful laughter, whirling toward them with a wide-eyed expression. "Is that right? Okay, well, how about this for a theory? Maybe you murdering bitches are the real reason we're here tonight. Maybe it doesn't have a damn thing to do with what happened senior year."

Tina gave him a look of withering disdain, shaking her head slowly to indicate how stupid she thought he was being. "And maybe you need to lay off the firewater. Our extracurricular activities have nothing to do with the rest of you. The senior year connection is the only thing that makes sense."

Belatedly noticing the wine dribbling from her glass, Colette corrected her loose grip on it and refilled it from the rapidly diminishing first bottle. "Jane the Ripper has a point, Bradley. On both counts, actually." She thumped the bottle down on the table and turned to look at them. "It's something to do with all of us. Otherwise why taunt us with poor Jake's stocking? Also, you never held your liquor very well. Not back in high school and definitely not now." Her laughter then had an almost cruel edge to it. "Hell, if not for you and Jake being drunken louts that long ago night, that terrible thing might never have happened."

Bradley's face reddened as he glowered at her. "You bitch."

Colette smirked. "You keep calling me that, like it means something to me. As if it might wound my fragile little feelings. I'm a lot tougher than I look, dear. Perhaps you should be careful what you say to me."

Bradley frowned. "That sounded a lot like a threat."

Colette shrugged. "Did you notice how my table had two place settings despite no one accompanying me to this dinner that never happened?"

Bradley's frown deepened. "What is this, some kind of fucked-up, pointless math problem? Why don't you just come out and say what—"

"There was never going to be a dinner."

The sudden intrusion of Harlan Ross's voice provoked a startled gasp or two. Until then, no one had taken note of his return to consciousness. He groaned and tentatively stretched his arms as he sat up straighter in the chair. Wincing, he pulled the sticky napkins away from his blood-smeared abdomen and spent some moments examining the small holes in his flesh. A small amount of blood still oozed out of the wounds, but the bleeding rate had slowed considerably. He pressed the napkins against his flesh and groaned again.

"Oh, that stings."

Nina put herself in front of him again, kneeling slightly at the waist with a concerned look on her face. "How do you feel?"

He grunted. "Like I've been stabbed three times by a lady who was not what she seemed. Other than that, peachy."

Nina laughed and glanced back at the others. "I think he's gonna be okay."

Colette smirked. "Yes. Thanks to having all that spare blubber to absorb the brunt of those vicious little jabs."

Bradley guffawed, shaking his head. "What did I tell you? A dyed-in-the-wool fucking bitch."

Tina groaned loudly in disgust. "Shut up, both of you." She turned away from them, training her gaze on Harlan. "What do you mean there was never gonna be a dinner?" She flitted her hand about in a general way. "Look at this shit. It sure as hell looks set up for dinner."

Harlan winced again and nodded. "Nothing more than stage dressing. The necessary elements of a scene our deranged hostess wished to enact. A scene like something out of movies we've all seen, old mystery novels we've all read. One ingrained with certain expectations she hoped to exploit to some unknown end. Only she didn't like the way things were going and abruptly quit in a rage."

Bradley came closer, nodding now, a lot of the angry red shade having drained from his features. "Yeah. You're right. It was like that. Like a kid frustrated by a video game."

Even Colette seemed ready to cease the verbal sniping in favor of reasoning the situation out in a calmer way. "Okay. Let's say that woman really is the brains behind all of this. If we ruined her fun somehow, what does she do with us now?"

Before anyone could answer, the lights went out again.

TWENTY

AT HIS SISTER'S DIRECTION, BERNARD Thornton leaned across his control console and flipped the switch to douse the lights in the dining hall. Above the console was an array of monitors displaying images from various locations throughout the manor. The speakers in the control room were currently tuned to the dining hall. As soon as the lights went out, the startled gasps and panicked shouts of the guests emerged from the speakers with the expected crystalline clarity of a state-of-the-art monitoring system.

Bernard leaned back in his swivel chair and laced his stubby fingers behind his head as he grinned at his sister. "You keep making moves like that, they're gonna figure out they're being watched."

Eileen snorted. "If they haven't figured that out by now, they're even stupider than I thought."

On a desk adjacent to the control console was a walkie-talkie. She picked it up, thumbed a button on the front, and alerted Janine about the move. "Clear the hallway of personnel," she went on, her gaze still on the dark screen of the dining hall monitor. She smiled as sounds of panic continued to emanate from the speakers. "Send everybody underground and keep them there until further notice. Let me know when it's done."

A silent beat elapsed.

Then Janine's voice came crackling back over the walkie-talkie's tinny speaker. "Yes, ma'am. Should take no more than five minutes."

Eileen returned the handheld unit to the desk and pursed her lips as she continued staring at the darkened monitor.

Bernard's hands came away from the back of his head as he leaned over, made a repulsive sound of dredging up phlegm from deep in his throat, and spat at a waste can overflowing with junk food wrappers and crushed soda cans. The dark-tinged wad of saliva and phlegm missed the can entirely and splashed against the wall behind it. The many dark stains on the wall indicated this was not a rare occurrence. Those stains, however, constituted just one part of a larger mosaic of filth. Another example was the bloody mess on the floor several feet to Eileen's right. Stephen Bain's corpse was gone, but the gory evidence of his violent demise remained. Someone would have to be sent up here with a mop and bucket, because otherwise the puddles of sticky blood and brain goop weren't going anywhere.

None of this was unusual for her brother. He'd reveled in his many disgusting habits since early childhood. Cleaning up his own messes was a habit he'd never acquired. This was why she never thought of him or addressed him by his given name. For decades now, she'd only thought of him as Trog. It'd started out as a disparaging nickname, but after a few years of relentless use by his sister, he'd simply given in and started answering to it. By then, no other surviving relatives remained to scold either of them for it. At this point, over twenty years after the death of feeble old Aunt Catherine, Eileen often wondered if he even still remembered his birth name.

Trog licked his chapped lips and snorted in a phlegmy way again. Then he reached into his loose sweatpants to adjust his balls. After tugging at his genitals a time or three, his hand stayed down there while he looked at his sister and said, "So why send the peasants underground? What are you planning?"

Eileen's nose crinkled in distaste. "Could you please take your hand out of your pants? I can see you fiddling with your balls."

Trog shrugged. "You're not the boss of me. I'll do what I want."

His hand stayed where it was. The ball-fiddling became more pronounced out of sheer spite. Eileen could only hope he wouldn't pull down his pants and begin openly masturbating in front of her. It'd happened before, though the last time was a good while ago. He'd stopped after she threatened to have him restrained while she took her time turning his junk to bloody mush with a hammer. As with so many other times she'd threatened him with punishment for his vile behaviors, he always reverted to bad habits after a while. He would either decide the threat wasn't serious or the passage of time simply scrubbed it from his memory. Given his penchant for huffing various toxic substances never intended for human inhalation, either possibility seemed just as likely.

"I can still get out the hammer and have some of my people hold you down."

Trog blanched a little at that. "You wouldn't."

"Wanna bet?"

Trog stared at her silently a moment, his eyes assessing. Then he sighed and slowly took his hand from his pants. "You can be really mean sometimes."

Eileen rolled her eyes. "I don't care what you do when you're not in my presence, but would it kill you to stop being such a perv in front of your sister?"

Trog huffed and looked away from her. "Whatever. You still haven't explained your next move."

"I'm letting them out of the dining hall."

Trog's gaze came back to her. "What for?"

She smiled and got a faraway, dreamy look in her eyes. "I'm going to do something I haven't done in a while. Let them have some time to roam around and look for a way out of Raven's Reach, which they won't find. Then, when I'm ready . . ." Her smile broadened as she pictured it in her head and found the prospect thrilling. "I'll go out there and hunt them down one by fucking one. Kill them all myself."

Trog grunted. "Ah. The slasher scenario. When was the last time you did that?"

Eileen frowned as she thought about it. "Hmm. Pretty sure it was that second group in 2017. You know, those ski club idiots."

Trog laughed and scratched his balls through the front of his sweatpants. "Yeah, yeah, I remember them." He was grinning, getting excited about the memory. "You even let me do one myself. That one blonde lady who looked like a *Playboy* centerfold." His grin faded as his features took on a pleading cast. "Could I do one this time, too? Maybe one of those sexy sisters?"

Eileen sighed. "I don't know. I'll have to think about it."

She had no intention of letting her idiot brother go after any of tonight's guests himself, mostly because she was still reeling from the disappointment of not getting to play out the long-planned scenario involving the fictional middle-class family in the way she'd hoped.

Over a year of work had gone into that. All for nothing now. All because of that loudmouthed bitch Nina Martinson. That level of crude bluntness in a social setting was not something Eileen had expected. The same went for those inconveniently intuitive insights.

Eileen knew she shouldn't be too hard on herself, though. A lot of what had gone into the planning for tonight was undeniably brilliant. She'd pulled off some audacious scenarios in the past, but the creation of the Dozier family far and away surpassed everything else. The easy part was hiring the supporting actors to play the kids. They were good enough to come off as believable in the situation, and the girl in particular was skilled at conveying what felt like genuine innocence and vulnerability. Eileen's own acting skills were unparalleled from years of immersive experience, which allowed her to work with the kids in a way that felt effortless. Until tonight, that is, when everything blew apart in a shockingly short amount of time.

The weak link was always going to be Alan Dozier. That wasn't even his real name. His real name was Russell Rigby. Russell was an insurance sales agent from Boise. He was a widower who'd lost his wife and two children in a tragic traffic accident just a few years earlier. This made him susceptible to brainwashing techniques at a level far exceeding that of the average person because there was already a deep yearning to deny the reality of the tragedy. His fragile mind was essentially rewired, suppressing all memories of his family's tragic fate. In their place came a fresh set of memories, implanted ones about a new family, one similar enough to the old one that imprinting their fictional history on his consciousness was easy.

The final phase was a week of immersive living with the reconstituted family. A suitable house was located and dressed up on the inside to give it a lived-in feel, including a Christmas tree to match up with the forthcoming holiday. Russell was taken there and removed from sedation. When he woke up, he believed it was just the start of yet another in a long string of ordinary days with his wife and kids, who were actually Eileen and the actors she'd hired. Each subsequent day unfolded in a way that effectively mimicked long-established routine. At no point did Russell show any signs of doubting his new reality. When the time came for the family to begin their journey to Raven's Reach, all seemed perfect.

Until, suddenly, it didn't.

Even at an advanced level, brainwashing was subject to falling apart if things occurred to plant seeds of doubt in the subject. When

Nina Martinson wouldn't stop prattling on about the actors not resembling Russell, Eileen knew it was only a matter of time before the man's false memories would start to crumble. A surge of uncontrollable rage caused her to abruptly terminate both Russell and the carefully crafted scenario. While it was possible she might have acted too rashly, there was nothing to be done about it now except adapt to the changed circumstances and try to make the best of it.

A crackling sound came over the walkie-talkie's speaker. "Hey, boss. Janine here. Everything's set."

Eileen didn't bother sending a reply.

Still looking at the dark monitor, she told her brother, "Hit the lights and open the doors in there."

Trog leaned over the console and started flipping switches. The monitor linked to the hidden camera in the dining hall brightened again and the speakers in the control room again erupted in a jumble of confused voices and sounds. Brother and sister listened in on their guests for a few moments, until Trog lowered the volume in response to a gesture from Eileen.

"What's up, sis?"

Eileen had a pensive look on her face as her gaze shifted to another monitor. "Let's cut Natalie Bain loose, too."

Trog looked surprised. "Really? I thought you had bigger plans for her. Long-term ones."

Eileen shrugged. "I did, but I'm still pretty miffed about my other plans going down in flames. Let's just add her to the mix and see what happens. Could be interesting if she meets up with the cool club. Then in the new year we can start over with a clean slate and start planning something bigger and better."

Trog got up from his chair, snagged his black hood and robe from a hook on the door, and started putting them on. "Makes no difference to me. I'll go let her loose. You ready?"

On the dining hall monitor, the surviving members of Stockdale High's Kool Klub of 1999 were still debating their next move. There was a lot of disagreement and hostility in those raised voices. In their senior yearbook, there was a full-page photo of all of them mugging for the camera. The words "Kool Klub" were splashed across the top of the page in a cartoonish font. A year ago, Eileen randomly found the picture while looking for inspiration for new Raven's Reach scenarios online. It was on one of those sites dedicated to helping former classmates reconnect. Deducing that they were the most popular kids in their class wasn't that difficult. She'd hated them on sight.

Eileen sighed. "Yeah. I'm ready."

Out in the hallway, after Trog locked the door and they started walking away from the control room, she glanced at her brother and said, "What do you think's up with all that cryptic shit they keep going on about? That solemn vow and all that noise?"

"Not sure," Trog said, grunting as he opened his robe and reached into his sweatpants to adjust himself yet again. "But it almost kinda sounds like they killed somebody a long time ago."

TWENTY-ONE

WHILE IT WAS TRUE THAT the wounds to the lower left quadrant of his abdomen were not leaking blood as profusely as before, the pain there was considerably greater than Harlan was letting on. He believed nothing absolutely vital was lacerated, because otherwise the pain would be close to unbearable, but what he *was* experiencing was bad enough. He'd love nothing more than to swallow several strong painkillers and spend the next several hours lying in bed. Under the present circumstances, however, that wasn't an option.

He heaved himself out of the chair when the lights came back on and clenched his teeth against the pain as he lurched his way over to the table to his immediate right. Grabbing one of the bottles left there by Bradley Winthorpe, he tore off the plastic seal at the top and removed the cap. He was taking his first big slug of whiskey when he heard a loud pop, a sound he subsequently realized was that of the dining hall doors being remotely unlocked. More whiskey was sliding down his throat when he saw the roll door go shooting upward.

Taking the bottle away from his lips, he wiped his mouth with the back of a hand and stared out at the section of empty hallway visible from his current vantage point. Of the hooded cretins who'd herded them into the dining hall earlier, there was no sign, but they might yet be lurking slightly out of view. The arguing voices of his companions were nothing more than white noise to him in those moments.

Anything they had to say was likely to be of little practical use. Any hope he had of surviving this night rested solely on his shoulders.

After bracing himself with one more big gulp of whiskey, he clenched his teeth and started lurching forward again. One of the Martinson sisters called out to him in alarm as he passed beyond the circle of tables and kept going. After that, he sensed the rest of them following at a cautious distance. Bradley asked him what he thought he was doing. The tone of cowardly fear rankled, as always. Even back in their high school days, he'd often sounded like that when faced with a tough situation, perhaps never more so than on that Christmas night twenty-one years ago.

Harlan's instinct was to hesitate as he arrived at the exit out to the hallway, but it was his intense dislike for Bradley that kept him going. He didn't want to ever think of himself as being even remotely like that contemptible fool. Not one of them—himself included—could ever be absolved of responsibility for their role in that tragic event all those years ago. Each of them owned some level of guilt for their abysmal behavior on that night. Yet, what Colette had implicated earlier was the absolute truth. If not for the reckless behavior of Bradley and Jacob Martinelli, it would never have become anything more than just another shameful bullying incident. No one would have died.

He stepped out into the hallway and stared down the long passage out to the foyer. At first he just stood there, staring straight ahead and saying nothing. A chorus of voices from inside the dining hall cried out for information. More white noise imbued with naked desperation. He raised the whiskey bottle to his mouth and took a long, slow swallow.

The hallway was empty.

He marched back into the dining hall and into the middle area between the circle of tables. Setting the liquor bottle down, he snatched his shirt off the floor and pulled it on, leaving it open in front. The lower left portion was sticky with his blood, but he would need a shirt if he managed to escape the manor. From what he'd glimpsed of the environs through the window in his room earlier, it was a cold and snowy evening. He didn't want to get hypothermia. Ideally, he wouldn't set out in search of help without a heavy jacket, but the shirt would be better than nothing. He found another stack of the thick dinner napkins, pressed them against the leaking holes in his flesh, and buttoned up the shirt, tucking it in as tightly as he could.

Then he grabbed the liquor bottle and started back toward the hallway.

Before he could reach it, Nina Martinson stepped in front of him and put a hand against his chest. "Whoa. Hold on there. We need to talk about what we're doing."

Harlan smiled. "I appreciate the kindness you and your sister have shown me. Truly. Though that in no way alters my opinion regarding your transgressions against humanity, your words tonight have touched me. Despite everything, there's a part of me that does still care for you both." His sigh then was imbued with palpable sadness. He gently took her hand from his chest and kissed the back of it. "There is, however, nothing for us to discuss. The rest of you can talk and strategize to your heart's content. In my view, the situation is simple. The disappearance of our adversaries may be temporary. Any time not spent trying to smash our way out of here is time wasted."

He released her hand and marched back out to the hallway. Finding it still empty, he continued down the long passage without breaking stride. He willed himself to move faster. The greater level of physical exertion worsened the pain in his abdomen, prompting him to take another deep swig from the whiskey bottle gripped tightly in his right hand. Aside from the liquor providing the only meager means of numbing the pain currently available to him, bringing the bottle along served another purpose. Even empty, it would have quite a heft to it. In a pinch, it would serve well as a means of bludgeoning an opponent.

He'd taken several long strides in the direction of the distant foyer when he heard the rest of his former classmates come skidding into the hallway as they raced to catch up to him. This was expected if not entirely welcome. There was no comfort to derive from the company of former friends. Not in this case. These people were uncomfortable reminders of a shameful phase of his life. Of the surviving members of the Kool Klub, the only ones for whom he still felt any small level of affection were self-confessed serial killers. As far as Harlan was concerned, that about said it all. While Bradley and Colette might not have killed anyone else in the intervening years, their souls were just as corrupted. They carried the taint of it around like a malignant dark aura.

Bradley Winthorpe fell into step next to him. "You're being a bit rash, aren't you?"

Harlan didn't bother looking at him. His view of the foyer continued to improve as he advanced rapidly down the hallway. From what he could see, it was just as devoid of manor staff. Gooseflesh speckled his arms. It felt colder in this passage than it had earlier. He quickened his pace and kept staring straight ahead as he said, "What makes you say that?"

Bradley huffed in exasperation. "Could you slow down? Maybe even stop so we can spend one goddamn minute talking this out?"

"No."

Bradley made a louder sound of irritation. "That other door was open, you know. The one in the back corner of the dining hall? I took a quick peek. There's a vestibule and then another door beyond that. Looked to me like it led to a big kitchen. We could've looked for things to use as weapons in there. Knives, meat cleavers, that sort of thing."

Harlan grunted. "You could still do that. Just turn around and head back. Nothing is stopping you."

The next few strides down the hallway passed in silence. Harlan didn't need to hear the man say it to know the truth. The prospect of going back to check out the kitchen unaccompanied was a terrifying one for Bradley. The hooded servants could be lurking anywhere and he would not want to risk facing any of them on his own.

"You don't like me much, do you, Harlan?"

"I do not."

Bradley made a dismissive sound. "Judgmental ass."

A wide range of scathing retorts occurred to Harlan but went unspoken. He didn't wish to waste even one more breath on this idiot. Besides, the foyer was only another several strides distant at that point. He could see almost all of it now, including one surprising detail that made his heart quicken.

The front door was standing wide open.

Obviously, this was why it felt significantly colder in the hallway now. Through the open door, he glimpsed snowflakes swirling in the night. Some of the snow was even coming through the open door, the flakes melting shortly after touching the marbled floor, which suggested the door hadn't been open for long. A faint level of exterior lighting was also visible through the open door.

As they emerged fully into the foyer, Harlan craned his head around, looking for any signs of lurking servants. His roving gaze took in the dual spiral staircases and the second-floor landings beyond. He saw no one. That did not, however, mean they weren't being watched. He imagined a room somewhere in the manor that functioned as a kind of nerve center, one equipped with banks of monitors displaying a view of every room in the place. The theory didn't come out of nowhere. The closed-circuit broadcast they'd all watched in their rooms earlier made it seem a likely possibility. Even now, someone was probably sitting in that nerve center, watching and waiting to see what they would do next. Because to whoever had summoned or brought them here, this was all a twisted game. A show or play of sorts, one in which the blood and bodies of the players were real.

Harlan slowed his pace considerably as he moved deeper into the foyer, head still swiveling about as he looked into the darkened offshoot passageways leading into other parts of the manor. Again, there was no hint of anyone lurking in those dark spaces, but those shadows felt alive with evil potential anyway.

In the middle of the foyer was a little round table. Arranged carefully on its surface were five more of those cheap, chintzy stockings with names spelled out in glued-on glitter. Despite his bravado of a few minutes ago, Harlan felt jittery with apprehension as he approached the table. The others followed his lead and crowded in close as they gathered around the table.

The names on the stockings were as expected—Harlan, Tina, Nina, Colette, and Brad.

Each name was struck through with a large black X. At the bottom of each stocking was a noticeable bump. No one felt the need to dig into their stocking and extract the lump of coal inside.

Nina hugged herself and shivered in the deepening cold. "So fucking creepy. And if *I* think it's creepy, I can't imagine how the rest of you feel. Guys, fuck this. We need to get out of here *pronto*."

She moved away from the table and started heading toward the open front door. Harlan's gut churned. Something didn't feel right. Something beyond everything he already knew. He turned away from the table and was on the verge of calling out to Nina as she arrived at the threshold.

Before any words could come out of his mouth, something snapped her head violently backward and an instant later the triangular wedge of an arrow head emerged from the back of her skull, dripping gore.

TWENTY-TWO

THE WOMAN WHO BELIEVED HER name was Alexandra Harcourt was feeling troubled. Her mind kept replaying images of Stephen Bain's head splitting open under the force of a heavy blade. The man's violent murder was a shocking and unexpected thing and its effect on her psyche was considerable. She feared whoever had killed her former stalker might soon do the same to her. Every faint noise from outside her room made her shiver and whimper in terror.

In other moments, when she was slightly calmer, she kept thinking about how all she wanted was to go back to her normal, boring life. The one where she lived alone in a small apartment and worked in a customer service call center, a dead-end job that was in no way gratifying but paid the bills. A lonely and sometimes sad life but a peaceful one. There'd been a certain amount of dissatisfaction in that existence, but she'd happily spend the rest of her days mired in go-nowhere boredom over what she was experiencing right now.

Also, as the minutes continued to tick by, she found herself becoming more overtly emotional every time she thought of that big blade bisecting Bain's handsome face. Tears welled in her eyes and spilled down her face in an almost continuous stream. What felt odd about this was the realization her tears weren't just about a fear for her own safety. That was certainly a factor, but some of what she was feeling was undeniably sorrow for Bain. Maybe something even deeper than sorrow.

Something close to grief.

For obvious reasons, this was deeply confusing. She could understand feeling sorry for the man on a basic human level. His history of being a harasser couldn't be forgotten, but as far as she knew, he'd never killed or physically harmed anyone. He wasn't a saint, obviously, but he hadn't deserved to die like that. Feeling bad for him for being terrorized and savagely executed made sense.

Grief did not make sense.

Grief was reserved for people you loved. Family and close friends. People with whom one shared a bond of profound intimacy. How could she be feeling anything of the sort for someone who'd once made her life so miserable? A man she hadn't seen or talked to in so long? She had no answer to those questions, but the intensely real anguish she was experiencing didn't care if she understood it. It just kept coming and getting worse. She was no longer just crying. She was sobbing, almost wailing with the horrific realization of an aching emptiness deep in her soul.

An emptiness that somehow felt connected to Stephen goddamn Bain.

Before she could spend much more time attempting to puzzle out the mystery of her feelings, a sound from out in the hallway caused her breath to catch in her throat. When the sound repeated and grew louder, she choked back another sob and blinked away the tears. She'd heard this sound before, ahead of her strange visit from the hooded man. Those same heavy footfalls. Was he coming back to ogle her naked form and masturbate under his robe again? Or was he returning for a more sinister reason?

The footsteps stopped.

A key rattled in the lock.

She stood up and backed away as the door swung slowly inward. Illumination from the hallway painted a slanting sliver of light on the hardwood floor of the room. Then the person who'd unlocked the door gave it a harder shove, making its hinges creak loudly as it swung all the way open, revealing a bulky, hooded form standing there framed in the brighter light from the hallway. Alexandra's heart raced and she had to swallow a sudden thickness in her throat. She trembled as she took some more backward steps.

She sniffled and shook her head. "Y-you better not lay a f-fucking finger on me, you son of a bitch."

The man in the hood laughed softly as he took his first menacing step into the room. "You dumb bitch. You think I'm here to hurt you?" Another laugh, this one tinged with mockery. "Do you really think you could stop me if I was? You're just a woman. Fragile. Weak. Pathetic. We both know I could have my way with you and you wouldn't be able to do a damn thing about it."

A ring with keys attached was looped over the forefinger of his right hand. As the man came slowly closer, he flipped the keys back and forth. A couple of those keys—old-fashioned ones—were distinctly longer than the others. Alexandra wondered if she might be able to snatch the keyring away from him and jab one of those longer keys through one of the eyeholes in his hood. Gouging or even piercing one of his eyes wouldn't kill the man, but it might disable him long enough to get herself loose. Of course, she'd be gambling on one of those keys fitting the lock in the cuff around her wrist, but that was a chance she'd have to take.

The man in the hood abruptly stopped approaching. He also stopped flipping the keys back and forth. "You're thinking about grabbing these, aren't you?"

He raised the keys and gave them a jangly shake.

"No."

The man laughed. "Liar. Your eyes were locked on them like a fucking laser. But, see, this is why I called you a dumb bitch. You think you know what's happening here, but you don't. The truth is, I've come to let you go."

Alexandra frowned. "Bullshit. You're just messing with me. Again."

The man shook his head. "Nope. I get why you'd think that. You're here against your will. A prisoner. As for messing with you . . . well, shit, we've been doing that for a long time. Longer than you'd ever guess. In ways you'd never guess. So you doubting my word makes total fucking sense. But I shit you not, I'm about to cut you loose of that chain. For real."

Alexandra was confused. "Okay. So what happens then? You just lock me in here?"

Another shake of the hooded man's head, followed by a chuckle. "Actually, no. I'm gonna walk out of here and leave that door wide open. What happens after that will be up to you."

Alexandra didn't believe it and said so.

The man shrugged. "Believe what you want. It doesn't matter.

You'll see for yourself soon enough."

He started coming forward again.

Alexandra willed herself to remain where she was. Maybe this was exactly what she thought it was, just another way of torturing her psychologically. In that event, there'd be no telling what might happen in the next few moments. More psychological torment, perhaps even a physical assault against her body. Even the mere thought of the latter filled her with dread. An assault could come in the form of sexual violation, but there was also a chance the man was hiding a weapon somewhere in that billowing robe of his. If she just stood where she was and waited, she might not know until it was too late to avoid a killing blow. At least, unlike poor Stephen, she wasn't completely immobilized.

She frowned.

There it was again, more of that inordinate sorrow for Bain. Then she saw his face in her head again and it was nothing like that strained, terror-stricken visage she'd seen on the closed-circuit broadcast. It was also nothing like her old memories of him from when he'd been stalking and harassing her. That arrogant, insidious smirk was missing. Instead, he was happy and smiling, and there was something in his eyes hinting at an emotional connection. She was tempted to write this off as nothing more mysterious than a false perception produced by stress, but that didn't feel right.

Something bigger was going on here.

The hooded man stopped approaching when he was within a few feet of her. "Hold out your hand."

Still distracted by the jumble of confused thoughts bouncing around inside her head, Alexandra held out a hand.

The man groaned in an exaggerated way. "The other one, you idiot."

Alexandra blinked rapidly in distracted confusion before realizing her extended hand was not the one with a cuff around it. After cringing, she lowered her extended hand and held out the shackled wrist.

The man chuckled as he slid a key into the cuff lock. "Like I keep saying. Dumb fucking bitch."

He gave the key a twist and the cuff popped open. Alexandra snatched her hand away as soon as it was clear of the cuff. The man allowed the cuff to slip from his fingers and in a second it hit the floor with a metallic clink. Alexandra tensed, readying herself to fend off the assault she still feared might be coming, but all the man did was stand there a few moments longer as he looked her up and down.

He sighed. "I'd really love to spend some quality time doing every nasty thing I can think of to you, but that would piss my sister right the fuck off and that's never a good idea." He laughed as he turned his back on her and started moving toward the door. After just one step, he turned around again and she saw him lick his chapped lips through the mouth-hole of the hood. "Oh, one other thing. You know what I said about how we've been messing with you for a long time? Well, that's an understatement. Guess what? Your name isn't Alexandra. My sister made that up. Your real name is Natalie Bain."

The woman's mouth dropped open as soon as he uttered those last words. Not because it was any kind of audacious lie, as she might have suspected earlier. The truth about herself was locked away in an artificially suppressed section of her psyche, a truth that had started pushing its way back to the surface even before this vile man came into the room. All of it came exploding out of that hidden place in a disorienting rush. The staggering horror she felt in those moments was multi-layered and seemed to encompass everything about her life.

All of it was a lie.

The lonely existence as an anonymous apartment-dweller. The soul-crushing dead-end job. Nothing more than a mysteriously elaborate and cynical fabrication. Her name was Natalie fucking Bain. Stephen Bain was her husband of nearly fifteen years. He'd never stalked or harassed her. *She* was the one who'd pursued him in the beginning. They had a young daughter and lived in a beautiful house in a wealthy part of the suburbs.

She was a fucking *doctor*. A pediatrician.

And then it all washed right over her and all that was left was an incendiary rage as the man in the hood again turned his back on her. She went rushing at him and leapt up on his back, hooking her legs around him as she beat furiously at his face with her fists. He screeched in surprise and fright and started whirling rapidly around in a desperate attempt to dislodge her. The arrogance of the man further fueled her thirst for righteous vengeance. It was galling to think he could just drop the kind of bomb he had and walk away. What that said was he didn't take her seriously as a threat at all. He was comfortable putting his back to her, even with her unshackled and reeling from the horror of the knowledge engulfing her.

Well, fuck that.

She pushed a thumb and finger through the eyeholes of his hood and gouged deep into his eyes. He screeched again as he crashed against the TV and sent it tumbling over the side of the cart. Somehow he managed to stay upright. She continued digging at his eyes and it wasn't long before he was shrilly begging her to stop. She did not stop. In a few more seconds, her thumbnail pierced the surface of his right eye and pushed deep into the vitreous. Growing increasingly more desperate, the man tried smashing her back against the tall wardrobe. The impact hurt, but her grip on him remained tenacious. She tore off his hood and bit into his ear, feeling warm blood on her tongue as she tore away a chunk of it. The taste of his flesh on her tongue was foul and she spat it out, but the repulsion she felt in that instant was no match for her white-hot fury. She immediately bit off another piece of his ear and spat it out as well.

By then the man was howling in agony. She could feel his strength deserting him and in another few seconds he dropped to his knees. After unclenching her legs from his midsection, she got her feet firmly planted on the floor and again dug deep into his wounded eyes and felt more vitreous fluid and warm blood flow over her fingers. He sobbed and started begging again.

After allowing herself a moment to draw in a few big breaths, she gave the man a hard kick in the ass, causing him to flop forward, landing face-down on the floor. Instead of trying to get up, the man stayed where he was, mewling and clawing weakly at the floor.

She glanced over at the coiled length of chain.

It looked long enough.

Grabbing it, she pulled it over and dropped down atop the man, straddling his back. She wrapped the chain twice around his neck and started pulling it tight. He tried grabbing at it, but it was no use. She sneered in hatred and disdain as she continued pulling the chain tighter and tighter. Eventually the man stopped fighting her. Stopped making any sounds at all. She didn't relax her grip on the chain until his body went limp. A moment later, an awful stench filled her nostrils as his bowels let go.

She climbed off him and for a while just stood there staring at the corpse on the floor. For the first time in her life, she'd killed another human being.

On purpose.

And she didn't feel the least bit bad about it. Not with the gut-twisting image of her husband's ruined head still blazing in her mind. Tears again welled in her eyes. She wanted to scream.

INVITATION TO DEATH

But there wasn't time for that. That door was still standing wide open. Maybe she had no real hope of escaping this place. Letting her out of the room was just another twist in the sick game her captors were playing, but after taking one of them down, she felt energized and triumphant.

One way or another, she thought, *I'm getting out of here.*

That or die trying.

A check of the wardrobe turned up some clothes. She found some shoes on a shelf above the hanger rack. The dead man didn't have a weapon on his person, unfortunately, but she took his ring of keys.

At the doorway, Natalie Bain took a cautious look out at the hallway.

It was empty.

She took one more big breath and got moving.

TWENTY-THREE

THERE WAS A MOMENT OF stunned, disbelieving silence as Nina Martinson took a single lurching backward step away from the door threshold. The screaming started when she toppled over and fell dead to the floor. A reflexive scream of fright from Colette and a much louder ear-piercing wail of overwhelming horror and desperate denial from Tina Martinson.

Tina ran to her sister and dropped to her knees at her side. She grabbed her by the shoulder and gave her a shake, a pointless attempt to rouse her. Just as pointless were the words coming out of Tina's mouth. She was sobbing and imploring her obviously dead sister to please get up, along with exclamations about how her death couldn't be real. *This can't be happening! This can't be happening!* Over and over, as if it would make a difference.

Some wildly improbable things had happened since his arrival at Raven's Reach, none of which had thus far involved magical resurrections. Bradley doubted Nina would be coming back from an arrow that had gone *straight through her fucking skull.*

Harlan Ross moved closer to the surviving Martinson sister, but he exercised at least some degree of caution by not putting himself in front of the open doorway, thereby not making himself an easy target for the murderous archery expert apparently lurking somewhere just outside. He bent at the waist slightly and called out to Tina in urgent tones, imploring her to get to her feet and away from the door. When his words did not appear to penetrate the invisible wall of grief surrounding her, he started shouting at her.

Colette screamed again as another arrow came flying through the open doorway and punched into Tina's left shoulder, causing her to cry out in sudden agony and spin away from her dead sister. A third arrow flew through the opening and just missed hitting the side of Tina's head when the momentum of her spinning motion exhausted itself and caused her to fall forward to the floor. The errant arrow continued deeper into the foyer and missed impaling itself in Bradley's left leg by about half a foot.

Bradley whimpered in belated recognition of his close call. A voice in his head was screaming at him to drop to the floor, but he remained immobile, frozen like a goddamn helpless statue while Harlan ran to the door and slammed it shut. The big man turned the lock and backed away as yet another arrow drilled into the door, striking it with enough force for the arrowhead and several inches of stainless-steel shaft to appear on the interior side.

Tina was screaming at an even higher volume than before. The angle of her fall toward the floor proved unfortunate, as the nock end of the arrow embedded in her flesh hit a groove between marble tiles and pushed the arrow deeper into her shoulder. The triangular arrowhead emerged just above the protruding edge of her shoulder blade. She screamed at ear-piercing levels again as she fell onto her side, bending but not breaking the arrow shaft. Harlan grabbed hold of her and forcefully yanked her to her feet, prompting even more screams. He was still shouting at her and trying to get her to focus, telling her they needed to retreat deeper into the manor to seek shelter or an alternative exit elsewhere.

Yeah, good luck with that, Bradley thought. *Bitch has a giant Medieval-looking arrow stuck right through her.*

Getting her to calm down and think straight probably wasn't in the cards. The man wasn't wrong, though. They were sitting ducks in the massive foyer. Retreat was the only thing that made sense at this point. Colette came to a similar conclusion seconds later when someone on the other side of the door grabbed hold of the handle and gave it a shake, making it rattle in the frame. She let out a startled shriek and went flying up one of those spiral staircases. Bradley turned his head and watched her go, marveling at how fluidly she was able to vault her way up those stairs in high heels. Some of it was natural grace, he supposed, but a burst of terror-fueled adrenaline probably helped. He thought about chasing after her, but quickly dismissed the idea. By now he believed he'd probably be better off on his own. There was freedom in not being responsible for another person. Or not being dragged down by them, for that matter.

Take Harlan, for instance.

The fool was still trying to reason with a person beyond reason. He'd probably still be at it when the maniac on the other side of that door finally burst into the foyer.

Grimacing in frustration, Harlan glanced his way. "Help me with her!"

A slow smile stretched Bradley's lips. "I don't think so, asshole."

Harlan was outraged. "You son of a bitch!"

Still smiling, Bradley shrugged.

He supposed he *was* a son of a bitch. In a way, he guessed he'd known it most of his life. Or at least all the way back to senior year at Stockdale High, when his drunken belligerence ultimately led to the accidental death of a kid who was barely smart enough to spell her own name. Yeah, the whole group of them had participated in the relentless bullying, pursuing the girl across the frozen pond that night, but he was the one who'd really pushed it to the limit. Jake had egged him on more than the rest, but that was just Jake being Jake. Trying to impress him. Trying to be like him. The idiot.

Only a really rotten to the core son of a bitch could've done what Bradley did that night. Only a son of a bitch so wrapped up in and blinded by his own arrogance would wind up in debt up to his eyeballs to the mob.

"Good luck, Harlan. I think you're gonna need it."

Still grappling uselessly with Tina, the big man glowered at him but said nothing further.

Bradley took some backward steps.

Then he turned around and went racing back down the long hallway to the dining hall.

TWENTY-FOUR

NO CONSCIOUS THOUGHT PROCESS SENT Colette racing up the stairs and back down the eastern wing hallway toward the room where she'd spent the early part of the evening. Nothing at all resembling coherent thinking existed in her head during those moments. She was driven only by blind panic and instinct, manifesting in the form of an overriding need to get far away from the shocking and scary things happening in the foyer and to do so quickly.

Only once she was a good bit of the way down the hallway did she stop to consider what she was doing. There was a good chance the person who'd shot arrows into the foyer was the same person who'd invited them here tonight. Even if the archer simply worked for that person, odds were still good the murderer might eventually look for her here.

She slowed her pace as this realization took up residence at the front of her mind. The killer might not come for her first, but she couldn't operate under that assumption. She had to proceed as if he were right on her heels and make her decisions accordingly. There were a lot of other rooms up here, most of them probably unoccupied. She started trying doors as she continued down the hallway, but found them all locked up tight.

The door to her room was still standing open. It was just a few more doors down on the right. She continued trying the other doors as she neared it, unsurprised by then as each failed to open. As she reached the open door, she hesitated at the threshold, her gaze going to the end of the hallway. She saw a window set in the wall there. Though unobscured by a curtain or blind, its view of the darkness outside was in no way revelatory. To the right of the window was an open space, beyond which was probably either another stretch of hallway or a staircase leading to a different part of the manor.

While it was tempting to enter her room and hide in that big wardrobe, she knew it wouldn't be the smart move. She might wind up dead whatever she tried, but she also knew she stood a better chance of finding a more viable hiding place by looking elsewhere.

She took a steadying breath and began to move away from the threshold, picking up speed with each step she took. A faint sound from somewhere close behind her made her stop and glance backward. What she saw then was so unexpected and startling it caused her to lose her footing and take an awkward tumble. This happened so quickly she had no chance to brace herself or do anything else to mitigate the impact of the fall. She banged an elbow against the floor, crying out in pain as she rolled onto her back.

Raising her head, she looked down the hallway and saw George Barrington hanging off the frame of the door outside their room. His handsome face was streaked with blood and his head looked like it was trying to fall off his sagging shoulders. It kept dipping precipitously forward before abruptly snapping into an upright position. The overall look was that of a barfly struggling mightily to stay on his feet and walk out of his favorite watering hole after closing time. His bleary eyes looked ready to roll back in their sockets at any moment.

Shit.

Instead of killing him as she'd assumed, she'd merely knocked him unconscious by smashing the ceramic chamber pot over his head. Thinking back on it now, she realized that at no point prior to frenziedly shoving him under the bed had she bothered to check the man's pulse, an instance of shortsightedness that was unlike her. She could blame that on a number of things. The impulsiveness of the act and her subsequent state of panic. The large pool of blood that spread out around his head so quickly. These things disrupted her usual orderly thought processes, resulting in an uncharacteristic lapse. Understanding *why* the lapse had happened, however, made it no more forgivable in Colette's eyes. She'd planned every aspect of her husband's murder with such meticulous care, with such cold efficiency. When not a single thing went wrong after the plan was set in motion, she took great pride in her ability to concoct and execute so diabolically perfect a scheme.

This thing with George was the exact opposite of that. She understood now that it was an unavoidable side effect of allowing someone so volatile into her life. She succeeded in other endeavors when she was able to control all the elements of her environment. George was different. She'd allowed herself to believe she could blunt his rougher edges by making him so dependent on her, but that had backfired in spectacular fashion. Clearly she'd become a touch too arrogant in her thinking after getting rid of David so easily. In retrospect, it was easy to see the decision to come to Raven's Reach as another manifestation of that arrogance. Here was another situation in which she was not in control of her environment. There remained a strong chance she might die because of all these lapses. Furious with herself now, she swore she would do things differently from this point forward if she somehow got out of this alive.

Still holding onto the doorframe, George took another lurching step into the hallway. "Fuckin' bitch. You tried to kill me."

The words came out slurred. Colette needed a few seconds to decipher them.

She sat up, wincing again at the lingering pain in her elbow. "You sound brain damaged. Do you know that? I might have failed in my attempt to kill you, this time, but I don't think you'll ever be your old self again."

His face twisted in a snarl. "Fuck . . . you."

He pushed himself away from the doorframe and took a few staggering steps into the hallway. There was little evidence of anything resembling control over his movements. He'd relied instead on momentum from the push away from the door to carry him this far. If not for crashing into the opposite wall, he would have collapsed to the floor. By twisting about and putting his back to the wall after that moment of initial impact, he was able to stay on his feet, but it was clearly taking everything he had to keep it that way. It looked to Colette like his legs might drop out from under him at any moment.

A quick mental calculation also told her a shove away from the wall with a similar degree of momentum behind it would get him to nearly within grabbing distance of her ankles after his inevitable collapse to the floor. One side of his mouth quivered while he glared at her and appeared to make the same calculation. When their eyes met, she knew she would not survive if he managed to get his hands on her.

They moved in the same moment, her scooting backward as quickly as she could manage while George shoved himself away from the wall. He was able to put an extra bit of strength into it this time as he leapt toward her with his arms outstretched. After he hit the floor, the grasping fingers of his left hand were within a few inches of one of her heels. Other than the weakly clawing movement of his fingers, however, he was motionless for several seconds, and during that time Colette allowed herself the hope that the crash had robbed him of what little strength he still had.

Then he heaved a breath and laboriously raised his head off the floor. He sneered and again mumbled something mostly indecipherable but which was probably another misogyny-laden expression of his deep desire to end her life. Groaning with the effort, he heaved the upper part of his torso off the floor and propelled himself another few inches forward. Sweat streamed down his face as he did this, turning the dried blood caked along his jawline wet again and making it run down his neck. He looked like a ghoul from some old horror film, risen from the grave to seek vengeance against those who'd wronged him.

As he flopped down on the floor again, the tips of his fingers scraped against the sole of the shoe on her right foot. Realizing again how close she was to utter disaster, she pulled her foot back and launched it forward, kicking him in the face. She heard a crunch of cartilage as his nose yielded to the force of the blow. George screamed and rolled away from her as more blood streamed from his nostrils.

Colette again scooted backward, but this time she finally had the presence of mind to get to her feet after spending too much time distracted by George's flailing efforts to pursue her. Unfortunately, at the same time, George also found some new reserve of strength, one he was able to access only after having his nose broken, most likely. He grabbed at the wall and was panting heavily as he hauled himself into a sitting position.

He grinned and licked blood from his lips as he turned his head to look at her. "Almost had you."

Colette sniffed disdainfully. "I'm reminded of something my grandfather used to say. Close only counts in horseshoes and hand grenades. As I'm fairly certain you don't have any hand grenades handy, I don't think I have much to worry about from you at this point."

Still grinning, George kept his back against the wall as he summoned every remaining iota of strength and propelled himself upward. Though Colette still didn't believe he posed any significant threat, she began to worry slightly when he pushed himself away from the wall and stood steady on his feet in the middle of the hallway.

"Wrong again, bitch."

This time she understood him perfectly.

Fuck.

He took one careful step toward her and did not fall over, followed by another one. And then another. The extreme amount of effort he was having to exert to remain on his feet was clear from the sweat pouring down his face, but he no longer looked on the verge of imminent collapse. He wasn't magically all better, but it almost didn't matter. A burning need to get back at her was driving him, temporarily overriding the new limitations imposed on him by pain and blood loss. Colette doubted this new invigoration could last for long, but it wouldn't matter if she didn't hurry up and get the hell away from him. All he had to do was get her hands on her and she'd be finished.

He started coming at her a little faster.

She screamed as she whirled about and started running away from him. An enraged roar escaped his lips as his heavy footsteps pounded the floor in pursuit. Colette picked up her pace and, in a few seconds, arrived at the open space to the right of the window. In front of her now, as she'd guessed, was a staircase leading back to the first floor of the manor, some part of it she'd not yet seen. The upper portion of the staircase was visible from the light here in the hallway, but the lower part was cloaked in darkness. No lights were on down there. The darkness was intimidating, but venturing into it was preferable to waiting around for George to catch up to her.

She started down the stairs at a rapid clip and was perhaps a half-dozen steps down when she heard a roar of rage from somewhere above her. Squeaking in fright, she had to grab hold of the rail to keep her feet from betraying her. In about another second, her feet felt steady beneath her again, but before she could take another step down, something heavy slammed into her back.

It was George.

Probably knowing he had no hope of catching up to her thanks to the unsteadiness of his gait, he'd opted instead to hurl himself down the staircase. It was a last-ditch desperate move by a desperate man. A man who by now knew he was close to death but wanted to be sure he took her with him.

They crashed and tumbled down the stairs in an awkward tangle of limbs. At one point before they reached the foot of the staircase, Colette felt one of her wrists snap and knew a shard of bone was protruding through her flesh. Other injuries occurred along the way. A broken ankle. She lost some teeth when her mouth smashed against the edge of a step. While in the midst of it, the fall seemed to go on forever. It felt like being caught in an endless time loop in hell.

Then they hit the floor at the bottom of the stairs and it was over.

Colette whimpered in pain as she raised her head and looked at her ruined wrist. The hand looked as if it was only still barely attached to her arm. She tried flexing her fingers and screamed at the shock-wave of pain. The rest of her didn't feel much better.

Turning her head, she saw right away that George was dead. He'd landed right next to her. His neck had been snapped at a horrifying angle in the fall. There were windows in the large room, which let in enough moonlight for her to see his unblinking eyes.

She felt surprisingly little satisfaction at knowing he was dead, not when she was little better off. Given the wrecked state of her body, escape from Raven's Reach tonight was impossible. She'd need a lot of help to get out of here and clearly none was forthcoming. Dragging herself to some viable hiding place also seemed unlikely.

A shadow fell over her.

She turned her head and gasped when she saw the figure clad in black. Though she couldn't see the person's face because of the hood, the person's form framed in the moonlight was obviously feminine. Clutched in the woman's gloved hands was the handle of a double-bladed axe.

Colette raised her head and tried to wriggle backward. "Please," she said in a voice choked with tears. "Please. It was so long ago. None of us meant for it to happen. I didn't really even have anything to do with it. I was *just there*, for fuck's sake! It's not my fault."

A barely audible grunt came from beneath the hood. "Lady, I don't even know what the fuck you're talking about."

Colette screamed as the axe came arcing toward her neck.

The scream cut off as the heavy blade chopped through it and sent her severed head tumbling into the darkness.

TWENTY-FIVE

THE POUNDING ON THE DOOR stopped while Harlan was still trying to drag Tina Martinson away from her dead sister. Right away, the cessation of the aggressive battering struck him as an ominous development. That the archer was someone who either lived or worked at Raven's Reach seemed obvious, which meant he or she would have relatively easy access to other ways into the manor.

It made no sense to spend even one more moment lingering in the foyer. The large open space made them easier targets than paper ducks in a carnival shooting gallery. To the left and right of the foyer entrance were dark hallways extending along the front of the eastern and western wings of the manor. Getting to some hiding place elsewhere in the manor was still possible, if they got moving right now. It was a faint hope at best, Harlan knew, but one he infinitely preferred to not trying at all. Not trying was tantamount to surrender, a prospect for which he felt a deep and instinctive repulsion.

Regardless, he was at a point now where he faced a stark choice. He could either give up on Tina and seek shelter on his own, or he could try something drastic to snap her out of her state of denial. He grimaced as he pictured what he had to do in his head. Under ordinary circumstances, it was something he'd never consider. Not even for a fraction of a second. He sighed heavily, recognizing the futility of continuing to argue with her. She was still screaming and trying to twist out of his grip. Given another few seconds, she'd probably succeed.

Now or never, he thought.

He slapped her. Twice.

Tina stopped struggling and glared at him. "Did you seriously just smack me? Like I'm some kind of hysterical hussy out of a 40s noir movie?"

Her aggrieved tone made Harlan wince inwardly, though he kept his outer expression stonily stoic. "I apologize. Truly. But you need to accept that your sister is dead. There's nothing you can do for her. We need to find somewhere to hide and figure out our next move."

She surprised him by laughing. It was the way she laughed rather than the laughter itself that caught him off guard. There was no tinge of the mania one might expect in a person experiencing severe pain or emotional distress.

"Don't you get it?" she said, smiling sadly as fresh tears leaked from her eyes. "I'm already dead. If not from this . . ." She indicated the arrow still embedded in her shoulder with a tilt of her chin. "Then from losing her." Her gaze went briefly to Nina's unmoving form. "We did everything together. And I do mean *everything*."

In the subsequent silent beat that elapsed, her eyes communicated something Harlan believed he was interpreting correctly. An insight that somehow managed the feat of coming as a genuine shock while also making a twisted kind of sense.

She sighed as she read the look on his face. "Don't strain yourself from thinking about it too hard. We took a path in life that meant we couldn't trust anybody else. All we had was each other. Nina was my world. My whole life. I'm nothing without her. I'm begging you to please understand and let me go." Her expression hardened when he just stood there looking at her for another silent moment. "Leave. Go."

She came at him then, bracing her hands against his chest and giving him a shove.

He took a couple of awkward backward steps, just managing to stay on his feet. "Fine," he said, sighing. "I'll leave you." There was more emotion in his voice as he said this than he would've expected, knowing what he knew about the sisters. "But what will you do?"

Tina smiled again, but this time the strain in the expression was clear. Pain and blood loss were taking their inevitable toll. "The only thing I *can* do. Goodbye, babe." She started to turn away from him.

Then she hesitated, glancing back at him. "Nina and I went on to do some pretty fucked up things and never once felt bad about any of it. I still don't. Not even now. You know what I do feel bad about, even after all this time? That poor dumb girl."

Harlan nodded. "Yeah."

There was nothing else to say.

Tina turned away from him again and went to the front door. He wheeled about and started running as she began to undo the lock. The pain in his gut was severe as he plunged deep into the dark hallway to the left of the foyer entrance. He could feel fresh blood leaking from the holes in his abdomen, staining the fresh padding of napkins he'd tucked inside his shirt earlier. What he wanted more than anything else was a chance to pause and rest, but instead he willed himself to pick up the pace. He heard the hinges of the front door creak loudly as it came all the way open. Seconds later came a disquieting sound he now recognized as that of an arrow punching through human flesh and bone. Right on the heels of that came the sound of Tina Martinson's corpse hitting the floor.

Through all this, Harlan urged himself to be strong and smart, to not surrender to the weakness of fear, but his resolve had its limits. He couldn't help throwing a glance over his shoulder as a black-clad feminine figure came through the open door and stood there in the foyer a moment, staring quietly down at Tina's unmoving body. She was carrying a large bow and had a quiver of arrows strapped over her shoulder. Her face was hidden by a hood, but Harlan had a good idea who she was anyway.

The moment of distraction proved costly as his feet skidded on the slick floor tiles. He flailed about blindly in the partial darkness as he fell toward the wall to his right. His hand catching hold of a wall sconce was the only thing that kept him from taking a painful tumble to the floor.

When the sconce tilted downward, he feared it would soon tear free of the wall, unable to bear his full weight pulling down on it. Then he heard a *click* and the downward trajectory of the sconce stopped as it locked into place. Right after that a door-sized portion of the wall began to swing inward. Maintaining his rigid grip on the sconce a few seconds longer, he got himself fully upright again and peered into the opening in the wall. He felt a strange sense of stupefied wonder as he realized what he was seeing.

I'll be damned. A fucking secret passageway.

The narrow passage extended farther than he could see but featured some form of low-level lighting. After a few more moments of peering into it in amazement, his brain snapped back into gear, reminding him of the danger close behind. He glanced again in the direction of the hallway and saw the black-clad woman still standing over Tina Martinson. It was hard to tell for sure, but she did not appear to have noticed him yet. There was no time to think about his next move, only time to act.

He flipped the wall sconce up and slipped into the passage as the wall panel began to close.

~

Eileen Thornton was aware of Harlan's presence in the hallway to her left. Given the sound of his huffing and puffing and the slapping of his shoes against the floor, not hearing him would not have been possible. The man wasn't dumb. This was something he would've undoubtedly realized if not for his fear playing havoc on his judgment. She was watching him as his feet skidded and he grabbed hold of the sconce in a desperate, instinctive bid to stay on his feet. Not laughing when the wall panel began to open wasn't easy. He'd just happened to latch onto the one that opened the secret passageway. As soon as that happened, she knew there was no chance he wouldn't seek refuge in the passage.

So long as he believed he wasn't being observed, that is.

She redirected her gaze to the body of her latest kill before Ross could glance back her way. This would be perfect, if it worked out the way she hoped. Allowing him to think she was still gloating over Tina Martinson's demise might be all the incentive he needed to do as she wanted.

She smiled when she heard the wall sconce click back into place. After making herself keep her gaze on Tina's slack features a few seconds longer, she glanced down the hallway and saw no sign of Harlan Ross.

Laughing, she unclipped the walkie-talkie from her belt and radioed Janine Blankenship. She told Janine where Ross was and what she wanted to happen. Janine told her she'd take care of it and Eileen returned the walkie-talkie to her belt.

Still laughing, she started down the same stretch of hallway, soon passing the now closed wall panel Ross had disappeared through moments earlier. She kept going, eventually turning down yet another hallway branch, one that would soon bring her to her rendezvous with Colette Hammerschmidt.

~

Although it was relatively narrow by comparison with the wide main hallways of the manor, Harlan's initial assessment of the secret passageway was that it was sufficiently wide enough to comfortably accommodate his slightly-wider-than-normal girth. This proved true for perhaps the first dozen or so feet into the passageway, but after that it began to narrow by subtle degrees, eventually arriving at a point where he had to turn sideways and put his back against one of the walls to continue making progress.

The narrowing wasn't such that he feared becoming stuck or unable to continue. He still had a few inches of open space between his belly and the opposite wall. It stayed like that after at least a dozen more feet of progress. Worst case scenario, he'd have to stop and go back the way he came, but he hoped to avoid that. He had no idea what might await him at the end of this passage, but he already knew an exit back out into that hallway he'd left behind would almost certainly put him back in immediate danger.

The unknown versus the known.

Right now he favored the former.

One factor that *was* making things a bit more uncomfortable was the encroaching sense of claustrophobia. The armpits of his shirt were stained wet from sweat. More sweat poured from his forehead and temples as his breath fogged up his glasses. He removed the glasses multiple times and tried to clear the lenses with the unbuttoned collar of his shirt. They always fogged back over again within seconds. Nothing he could do about it. He kept inching along and working to hold back the claustrophobia, which had somehow reached the point of becoming intolerable without him even noticing.

A despondent whimper escaped his lips. He had no choice now but to turn back and take his chances in the hallway. Before he could do that, however, he became aware of what sounded like a faint grinding of hidden gears. Immediately after detecting the sound, the wall in front of him—already uncomfortably close—began to slide even closer. That sound of grinding gears got even louder.

Harlan yelped in fright and tried shuffling rapidly sideways back in the direction of the hallway. When he was unable to progress beyond the first few feet, he turned his head and was horrified to see that the passage back the way he'd come had also compressed to the point of being impassable. Tears joined the rivers of sweat as Harlan screamed and screamed.

The walls continued to compress.

Harlan became pinned, unable to move. He started mumbling prayers out loud, something he hadn't done since childhood. That grinding sound was louder than ever now. He feared it'd be the last thing he heard before being crushed to death.

But Harlan was not crushed by the walls.

Instead, a section of the floor opened beneath him and he screamed again as he dropped into a deep open place under the house. It was darker in this space and he never saw the crisscrossed strands of razor wire dozens of feet below. He felt that moment of excruciating impact, though. Fortunately for Harlan, however, the pain did not last long as his body was sliced into more than a dozen different pieces within seconds. His last conscious thought was of a girl falling through a hole in a sheet of frozen ice.

TWENTY-SIX

THE KITCHEN ADJACENT TO THE dining hall was even larger than Bradley had expected based on his earlier brief glimpse of it. There were multiple grills and fryers, along with several prep tables and two large sinks for washing dishes. If adequately staffed, it looked more than capable of servicing the clientele of a large and bustling restaurant.

From the look of things, however, a lot of years had gone by since the last time meals of any sort were prepared in this place. The fryers and grills were coated with a deeply encrusted grime. Bradley saw pots and pans randomly scattered about. Some were on prep tables, which at least made some level of sense, while others rested on the filthy floor. The sinks were piled high with dirty plates and dishes. It was markedly colder in here than anywhere else in the manor, further confirmation that no one had operated any of the ovens or other cooking equipment in recent history. He couldn't help wondering if any of it was still connected to electricity. He suspected not, given the disgusting state of things. This was a curious thing for at least a few reasons, but primarily because of at least one objective fact. There were several people who stayed at the manor on at least a part-time basis. They had to eat, right? So where did they take their meals? Where did they prepare them? Certainly not in this filth-ridden culinary graveyard.

These were questions without immediately obvious answers. His curiosity was slightly piqued, admittedly, but he didn't actually need answers. What he did need was a place to hide and some means of defending himself. In the interest of addressing the latter concern, he began opening and rooting through drawers. Some of the drawers were empty save for a few spider eggs and bug corpses. One drawer was filled with a number of random items, some of which were related to food preparation while others had no obvious business being stowed away here. An example of the latter was a raggedy Mickey Mouse doll that had seen better days. It was in there with an egg beater, a nutcracker, a paring knife, an assortment of forks and butter knives, a rolling pin, a cracked meat thermometer, and a single sealed condom that looked like it might have been new forty years ago.

Muttering in frustration, he slammed the drawer shut and entered a more manic phase of his search. He opened every remaining drawer and cabinet, hauling out their contents and dumping them on the floor. There was nothing of use anywhere. He even got down on his hands and knees and dug through the junk that was already there before he started adding to the piles of debris. After several frenzied minutes, it belatedly occurred to him that he was making a lot of noise and probably shouldn't be doing that. Also, the Armani suit was getting ruined in the process. Not that he actually cared. He was fighting to stay alive.

When he got to his feet again, he stripped off his suit jacket and tossed it away. His fingers worked fast as he undid the knot of his tie and removed it as well. He was on the verge of casting it aside when he hesitated, eyeing the long strip of burgundy-colored cloth in a newly contemplative way. There was a deadly potential in ties people didn't normally spend a lot of time thinking about. At least a few very famous people had gone to their deaths hanging from door knobs with ties knotted around their necks.

At no previous point in his life had Bradley Winthorpe ever seriously contemplated suicide. And why would he? He had money and nice things. Good looks that made hooking up with beautiful women whenever he wanted a snap. His attitude most of his life was that suicide was for losers and he was not a loser. Except now things had changed. Most of his money was gone. He was deep in debt to both the bank and the mob with no clear way out, especially now that he knew there was no million dollars to be won here. Suppose that by some miracle he *did* make it out of this place alive.

What then?

His troubles would still be out there waiting for him. A reckoning would come and he could imagine no realistic way of eluding it. A big breath pushed its way out of him and he suddenly felt exhausted and defeated. Maybe the only way out at this point *was all the way out.*

He'd never have to pay his debts. Never have to face the humiliation of becoming just another ordinary loser. Never have to drug himself into another dreamless sleep to avoid memories of that night on the frozen pond. The prospect of taking his own life—of potentially no longer existing in any form—remained a terrifying one. If he allowed himself to give it any real thought at all, he probably wouldn't be able to go through with it. The key to doing it successfully, then, must be to do it fast with little to no thought at all.

Bradley allowed his gaze to sweep around the kitchen until it settled on a large square-shaped skillet rack hanging from a rafter above one of the prep tables. The rack was ringed with hooks designed for holding pots and pans by their slotted handles. Only one rusted old skillet was hanging from one of the hooks. The rest were bare.

Don't think. Just do it.

He went to the table and climbed up on it. Instead of wrapping the tie around one of the hooks, he tied it around the metal frame of the square-shaped rack. Once it felt secure, he squatted on the table and looped the other end around his neck, cinching it tight. When that was done, he sat down and slowly slid his ass over the edge. With his feet not quite reaching the floor, the tie snapped tight.

His airway was cut off within seconds. Instinct caused him to kick and thrash as the terrifying reality of rapid air loss took hold. That terror in turn caused him to try to swing himself back onto the table. There was a moment there where he might have accomplished it with relative ease, but beneath the terror he felt, something else was at work.

Something cold and merciless.

A self-hatred more virulent than the deadliest of poisons.

He numbly pushed himself away from the table and within moments was close to losing consciousness. His vision blurred and he felt strangely light hanging there from the skillet rack, no more substantial than a feather floating in the wind.

Bradley closed his eyes and felt himself fading away.

He spent an unknown period floating in blackness.

Then consciousness returned and he found himself lying flat on his back on the prep table, staring up at the cobwebs in the corners of the kitchen's ceiling. Black spiders hung suspended in parts of the webbing. Some of them moved. He saw something else curious hanging above him—one half of his tie. The other half was still wrapped around his neck, albeit more loosely now. He gingerly touched his neck, wincing at the soreness there. He'd been cut down and laid out flat on the table by some unknown interloper. Maybe one of his old classmates had returned to save him from himself. That didn't seem likely, but in those first moments of foggy consciousness, he couldn't think of another explanation.

Then he became aware of a strange weight on his lap.

He frowned.

What the hell?

He raised his head and saw Colette Hammerschmidt's severed head resting on his crotch. His eyes bulged in their sockets, terror shooting through him like a lightning bolt. The urge to kill himself was wiped instantly away, as if it'd never existed at all. In that moment, all he cared about was saving his own ass and getting far away from whoever had done this to Colette.

A woman laughed from somewhere nearby.

He heard footsteps on the floor.

He sat up in time to see the blade of a meat cleaver arcing toward his face. There was no time to get out of the way or defend himself. No time to do anything other than think, *Where the hell did she find that fucking thing!? I looked everywhere!*

The blade of the cleaver chopped deep into his head.

EPILOGUE

CONTRARY TO WHAT WAS PUBLICLY "known" about Raven's Reach, the property had never fallen out of Thornton family hands. Instead, it was used as a place for conducting research across a broad spectrum of fields in which the eccentric family was interested, including many mainstream science and society would deem abhorrent. A lot of it didn't pan out, most notably an effort to restore corpses to life that spanned more than a century before being abandoned. The number of skeletons buried on the manor grounds and in the surrounding woods numbered in the hundreds. All sacrificed in the service of a line of research that ultimately failed to lead anywhere fruitful.

A parallel quest to refine and perfect ways of manipulating human minds, however, was far more successful. Techniques exceeding anything developed by U.S. or foreign intelligence agencies were created. Earlier generations of Thorntons used them to influence politics and society in ways that enhanced the family fortune and even occasionally did an actual bit of good in the world, if only as an unintended side effect.

By the time the twenty-first century rolled around, the Thornton bloodline had dwindled considerably. Once it got down to just Eileen and Bernard, all pretense of a higher purpose in the work done at Raven's Reach was jettisoned. With her hands finally on the purse strings, Eileen decided it was time to have some fun. She started devising her scenarios and using the limitless resources at her fingertips to bring them to life.

And now her latest batch of human playthings was down to just one.

Natalie Bain was waiting for her in the foyer. She'd removed an arrow from the corpse of one of the dead sisters with the apparent intent of using it as a weapon.

Eileen Thornton smiled as she came farther into the foyer, not stopping until she was within approximately six feet of the other woman. "What are you planning to do with that thing?"

Air hissed out from between Bain's clenched teeth. Her grip on the shaft of the arrow tightened noticeably, her knuckles turning white. "Kill you."

Eileen laughed.

She removed the hood from her head and cast it aside. "Why would you want to do that?"

Bain's face twisted in a bitter scowl. "You kidnapped me. Fucked with my head. Had my husband killed."

"Those things are all true." Eileen looked at the floor and made a tsk-tsk sound in her throat, one tinged with a regretful tone. Then she raised her head and smiled again as she met Bain's hateful gaze. "Or are they? Maybe you're confused. Maybe you don't know what you think you know. You're not Alexandra, but maybe you're not Natalie either. Maybe who you really are is buried too far beneath too many layers of fabricated realities to ever be found again. Or . . ." She stretched the single syllable out as she came another slow step closer and smiled more brightly than ever. "Here's a real mind-fucker of an idea for you to consider. Maybe you've never had a real name at all. Maybe you've spent your whole life locked up in a cell under this house, being endlessly experimented on while—"

Natalie screamed and lunged forward, ramming the blood-encrusted arrowhead deep into the hollow of Eileen Thornton's throat.

Eileen's eyes popped open wide, registering surprise.

She was so used to twisting people up with her words and getting under their skin she never viewed any of them as a real threat. Her jaw worked as she tried to speak, but the arrow lodged in her throat prevented any words from emerging.

Natalie Bain maintained her rock-solid grip on the arrow's shaft, holding it in place while Eileen's hands clutched weakly at it. A large amount of blood bubbled out around the arrow. Eileen's eyes opened wider, an attempt to silently project a plea for mercy.

Natalie sneered.

Then she ripped the arrow out of Eileen's throat. Eileen dropped immediately to her knees, several large gouts of blood spurting from the hole in her neck. She put her hands over the hole and more blood rushed through her fingers. In a few more seconds, she fell over and didn't move.

Bain stood there and stared at her a while longer, feeling more exhausted than triumphant.

A short time later, she let the arrow slip from her fingers and land with a clatter on the floor. She went to the front door and tried the handle, finding it unlocked. After opening the door, she shivered at the blast of cold air that rushed in. Hugging herself tight, she walked out into the cold and swirling snow.

~

Down in the underground facility, Janine Blankenship frowned as she stared at a black-and-white monitor and watched the woman go.

One of the other servants, a tall man with a livid scar running down one side of his face, was watching with her. "Jesus. I can't believe that bitch is dead."

Janine sighed. "It was a matter of time, I guess. She got too reckless. Too arrogant."

The tall man nodded. "Yeah. Too bad, though. That's the end of the gravy train for us. Should we stop Bain from leaving? Or Carol, or whoever the fuck she's supposed to be this week."

Janine thought about it. "Hmm. Not sure why we should."

"For revenge?"

Janine laughed. "Nah. Fuck it. Eileen Thornton was nothing but a paycheck to me. Besides, she was right about how messed up that woman's head is. She was locked up down here for years, you know, from long before you came on board. On the off-chance she's actually able to get off the mountain and make her way to town, she won't even remember this place by the time she gets there."

The tall man frowned. "Huh? How do you figure?"

Smirking, Janine tapped a finger against her right temple. "A failsafe wired into her psyche. Ms. Thornton did it to all her subjects. A better safe than sorry kind of thing, I guess. It was never actually needed until now. Once she's away from Raven's Reach, she'll forget it ever existed."

The tall man grunted. "Wow. Crazy shit. Anyway . . . I guess the rest of us should clear out now."

Janine turned away from him and crossed her arms tight beneath her breasts, smiling in an almost playful way as she said, "I guess we could do that. Unless . . ."

The tall man was frowning again. "Unless . . . what?"

Janine moved away from the bank of monitors and beckoned him to follow with the crook of a finger. The tall man hesitated for only a second before joining her just outside the medieval-looking cell currently housing the pretty young actress who'd played Kara Dozier earlier in the evening. Her actual name was Marnie Richardson, but perhaps she'd be getting a new one soon. The girl was curled up on her side, sleeping on an uncomfortable-looking cot.

"What are you thinking?" the tall man asked.

Janine nodded slowly to herself as she stared in silence at the sleeping girl a moment longer.

Yes, she thought. *I can do this. It's crazy, but I can totally do it.*

In her years of serving as Eileen Thornton's only trusted personal assistant, Janine had paid close attention to many things. She'd learned a lot and Eileen had never even noticed. And now all the Thorntons were gone. Dead. But Janine knew how to run everything at Raven's Reach. More importantly, she knew how to access the vast Thornton fortune. Until now, she'd never dared, but at this point there was nothing to stop her.

There was no reason she couldn't take over.

Completely take over.

She glanced at the tall man. "Have Ms. Wickman prepare the sensory deprivation chamber. And get somebody to bring me a laptop." An eager smile curled the edges of her mouth as her gaze returned to the sleeping girl in the cell. "And make it fast. I need to start writing a new scenario."

BIO

Bryan Smith is the author of numerous novels and novellas, including *68 Kill*, *Slowly We Rot*, *Depraved*, *The Killing Kind*, and *Kill For Satan!*, which won a Splatterpunk Award for best horror novella of 2018. He won a second Splatterpunk Award in 2020 for *Dirty Rotten Hippies and Other Stories*. He is also, along with Brian Keene, the co-author of *Suburban Gothic*. A film version of *68 Kill*, directed by Trent Haaga and starring Matthew Gray Gubler from *Criminal Minds*, was released in 2017. His favorite beers as of this writing are Zombie Dust pale ale from 3 Floyds Brewing Co. and Evil Octopus black ale from Mayday Brewery. He lives in Tennessee with his dogs Mac and Roxie.

Other Grindhouse Press Titles